THE BAT STAFFEL

By Robert J. Hogan

ALTUS PRESS • 2018

© 2018 Altus Press

PUBLISHING HISTORY

"The Bat Staffel" originally appeared in the October, 1933 (Vol. 1, No. 1) issue of *G-8 and His Battle Aces* magazine.

ALL RIGHTS RESERVED

No part of this book may be reproduced or utilized in any form or by any means, electronic or mechanical, without permission in writing from the publisher.

This edition has been marked via subtle changes, so anyone who reprints from this collection is committing a violation of copyright.

Visit ALTUSPRESS.COM for more books like this.

G-8 AND HIS BATTLE ACES:
THE BAT STAFFEL

CHAPTER 1
CONDEMNED TO DIE

EXCEPT FOR the ticking of the small watch on his wrist, the dungeon beneath Freiburg Castle was deathly still.

Tic, tac, tic, tac, tic, tac.

The watch seemed to clack faster with every complete turn of the second hand. Faster as though to betray its owner. To hurry the death that would surely be his within the next hour, perhaps the next few minutes.

The prisoner rose from his seat on a heap of human bones, yawned and stretched. In the dim gray light that filtered in through the slit two inches wide above his head he glanced at his watch. Nodded.

"Ought not to be long now," he ventured. "If I know human nature I'll win. If I don't—" he shrugged and drew his finger in significant gesture across his throat.

The voice of the prisoner, as he talked to himself, seemed far too young for the old peasant that he appeared to be. When thrust into the cell the night before he had been stooped and twisted with age. Now he stood erect. His face, still disguised with clever make-up, was the face of an old man. But the eyes were those of commanding youth. Gray, steel-hard eyes, they were. Eyes with magnetic power to hold others.

Unforgettable eyes.

G-8 AND HIS BATTLE ACES

The watch ticked on. Death came closer at every second. Arrested as a spy. Sentenced to be shot at one hour after dawn. But the young man disguised as a peasant smiled as he watched the light grow brighter through the slit above.

A moment later he laughed.

Facing death and this man could laugh.

But he was different from others. He was G-8, the young American spy. Germans lowered their voices when they spoke of G-8. Lowered their voices and cursed under their breath.

G-8 seemed infallible, hardly human in his super-skill.

One great general of the Imperial army had said:

THE BAT STAFFEL

"We must capture and kill this *verdammt* young man, G-8, at all costs. I would give willingly ten thousand of my bravest for his head. He is too clever to live. He knows more about our business than we do ourselves."

Now G-8 was held captive, but by his own planning. He had flown a Spad over the Swiss-Franco border the evening before, had landed in Germany dressed as a peasant, and when he could penetrate Freiburg Castle no farther had permitted himself to be captured by the strong guard.

Later, under rigid questioning by *offiziers* of the castle, he had permitted them to force an admission from him that he was a spy. But only on one condition would he tell them by what name he was known to the American Secret Service. So far the Germans had not complied with that request.

All this was part of a plan formed by G-8 to learn something that he must know. Something that was impossible to learn in any other way.

Footsteps sounded down the dank, musty corridor leading to his cell. Clanking steps of hob-nail boots.

"I'd give a hundred francs," G-8 said to himself, still smiling, "to have a picture of their faces when I tell them who I am."

A light shone through the grated hole in the great thick door. A round, close-cropped head appeared. Narrow eyes stared inside at G-8. Then a great rusty key grated in the lock. Hinges creaked and groaned as the door moved. A big German guard was straining at it with all his might.

G-8 had at once stooped over, assumed the pose he had had

the evening before when brought in. The old stooped peasant. Through the half open door two figures glided.

THE FIRST figure was a tall, slim, be-monocled German *offizier*. He gave a short nod of his clipped head.

Behind him came a chaplain carrying a black book.

The *offizier* spoke.

"You are about to die, *Mein Herr*," he said politely. "You will not tell us who you are?"

G-8 craned his head at the end of his thrust forward neck.

"I have given my answer to that," he said. "But in case you have forgotten I will repeat. You, *Herr Kapitan*, are only a tool in the hand of a master mind. Take me to your leader, your boss, your brains. The man who does your thinking for you. Tell him I have something of interest for him. Then and not until then will I disclose who I am."

The German *offizier* shook his head.

"I tell you, *Mein Herr*," he insisted, "there is no other in command here at Freiburg Castle other than I. *Versthen sie?*"

The *offizier* turned.

"I go now and leave you alone with the chaplain to prepare you for your death before the wall."

A cackling laugh came from the twisted lips of the peasant. G-8 waved away the chaplain with one hand, clutched the arm of the *offizier* with the other. He nodded to the astonished chaplain.

"It isn't that I do not honor your calling or my maker," G-8 explained. "It is that I am not ready to die. Not yet."

Still stooped he laughed up into the *offizier's* face.

THE BAT STAFFEL

"Get back, or I'll let this tank of poison gas go!" G-8 warned the German.

"Listen," he hissed. "You lie about the man above you. Go tell him for me that I have something to interest him concerning his tunnel through Switzerland."

The eyes of the *offizier* opened wide. His mouth dropped. He stared dumbfounded at G-8.

"*Gott in Himmel!*" he exploded. "You know—"

G-8 smiled.

"*Jawohl.* Either I know or I'm a good guesser. Go tell the big boy what I said and take this chaplain with you. He makes me nervous." He glanced at the slit above as the two moved toward the door. "And hurry. It's getting time for the shooting and I wouldn't miss that for a lot."

The two left hurriedly. The German *offizier* passed through the door behind the chaplain. He threw a last glance, a puzzled, questioning glance at G-8 as he went out.

The door creaked shut with the big guard straining upon it as he had done to open it. The key squawked and scratched in the lock. The sound of footsteps died away down the hall, then silence once more.

G-8 straightened, moved his shoulders to take the stiffness out of them. He was smiling as before. He broke into a laugh.

"Hope these Krauts don't think I came here deliberately just to be captured and shot," he said.

Minutes, two, three, four—then the clank of boots on the stone paving outside. Voices. The door swung open with the same groaning sound. The *offizier* came in, this time alone. He jerked his head toward the open door.

"Come!" That was all he said. But his face was white.

G-8 was stooped again. He moved toward the door with the shuffled walk of a cripple, passed out into the corridor. Out of the corner of his eye he saw the glistening blade of the bayonet on the end of the rifle that the big guard carried. The *offizier* was beside him, passed him and led the way down the dark passage.

He stopped before a niche in the wall, turned and pointed. G-8 could see a narrow staircase of partly crumbled stone leading from the dungeon corridor. The *offizier* jerked his head upward. G-8 began to climb.

THE BAT STAFFEL

Forty-seven steps he counted, then another corridor of stone. They stopped before a blank wall. The *offizier* was fumbling with something in the stone. Presently the wall moved. Part of it opened and disclosed a room beyond.

The *offizier* bowed, stepped aside and motioned G-8 to enter through the opening.

"You have asked to see his *Excellenz,* the *Herr Doktor,*" he said. "You shall see him."

"*Gut,*" nodded G-8. "That has been one of my greatest ambitions."

He stepped through the thick stone wall into the room.

INSTANTLY, G-8 glanced about him, tried to get his bearings. The room was not large. Empty book shelves told of this room once having been the library of the castle. Like all the rest of the Freiburg Castle that G-8 had seen, the place smelled musty and aged.

The *offizier* followed him into the room, and the door which closed behind him seemed lost in the side of the stone-walled enclosure.

For a moment they stood alone in the room. G-8 turned to the German beside him.

"How long will we have to wait for his *Excellenz?*"

A look almost akin to horror crossed the face of the *Kapitan.*

"It is," he said in astonishment, "not when we wish to see the *Herr Doktor,* but when he will see us. We must be patient. The *Herr Doktor* is a great man—and very busy."

The words had hardly left the *offizier's* mouth when a sound came from the far corner of the room. Even in the light that strained in through the high window across from where they stood, the corner from which the sound came was but dimly discernible.

G-8 was first conscious that someone else was in the room when he felt that third being rather than saw him. But almost instantly following that sensation came the quick strides of a small, wiry man.

He was short, slim, almost emaciated in appearance. His face was that of a homely, half-starved school boy in his early teens. His lips did not quite meet, and between them showed large irregular teeth, the two upper tusks twice as long as the others, protruding downward in hideous fashion.

His forehead was large. His whole head was oversized, with capacity for an enormous brain, and made more grotesque by being shaven clean. Fire seemed to dart from the tiny eyes, set close together, that peered through extraordinarily thick glasses. And when the man spoke his words came in a flat, high-pitched voice.

He thrust a long envelope of papers toward the *Kapitan* who had accompanied G-8 into the room.

"Here," the *doktor* cracked. "I have finished the plans. Take them at once to the one in charge. Heraus mit."

The little man jerked round suddenly as though he hadn't yet noticed G-8 standing there in the room. The *offizier* turned abruptly with the thick envelope. The side of the wall opened for him. He passed through.

G-8 tensed there for an instant. He might take a chance and leap through after the *offizier*. Might take those papers away

THE BAT STAFFEL

from him and get away with it. But he couldn't tell what the plans contained. If they were mere drawings they wouldn't help so much. He wanted to get information from the *doktor*.

And already the *Herr Doktor* was speaking to him. Speaking in that flat, high-pitched voice that shook with anger.

"And you," he cried, "who are you to demand to see Der great *Herr Doktor* Krueger? You who are about to die. What do you know about a tunnel through Switzerland?"

G-8 was still stooped, still in that twisted shape. He smiled. Smiled up at the *Herr Doktor*. For in his stooped position he was not as tall as the little scientist.

"I shall answer your questions backward," G-8 said calmly. "First you ask what I know about a tunnel through Switzerland." He jerked his head toward the place in the wall through which the *offizier* had departed. "Those plans were for the completion of that Swiss tunnel that will run into the valley of the Rhone, *nicht wahr?*"

The little *doktor's* eyes bulged. His mouth opened in a snarling pose.

"*Ach,* you know too much."

G-8 shrugged and his smile broadened.

"But not enough," he said. "It is strange, but one in my position, a man about to die before the firing squad, becomes curious at times about something that is not solved. Something that would go on a mystery to his soul forever were he to die before he learned of it. That is why I demanded to see you, *Herr Doktor* Krueger. Two so great as you and I should not part without understanding each other better. You, the master mind. And I, the master spy, so some say of me."

The little *doktor* blinked through his thick glasses. For a moment his ego was gone. White crept into his features for the briefest second.

"Master spy," he repeated. "It could not be. You? You are not—"

The corners of the young American's mouth twitched uncontrollably.

"If you're thinking of G-8," he said, "you're a good guesser."

But still he held his stooped position.

"Gott in Himmel," exclaimed the *Herr Doktor* Krueger and again in reverend, almost fearful prayer. *"Gott in Himmel!"*

BUT THE exclamation of the little *doktor* was not the only one that G-8 heard. There was a quick intake of breath in the dark corner from which the *doktor* had appeared. Then, for the first time, G-8 realized for sure that they were not alone, he and the *doktor*.

He squinted into the darkness of the corner, made out a big German there with a Luger in each hand. His hopes fell a little at sight of him. His voice when he spoke to Krueger was calm, sure.

"You see I thought you'd recognize the name," he smiled. "I might have sent my card in, but I wanted to see the expression on your face when you realized that you actually held as a prisoner of war G-8 himself."

The steel-gray eyes of G-8 were focused full on that childish face of the little giant of science. The master American spy never

THE BAT STAFFEL

missed the movement of a facial muscle nor the flick of an eyelash. His hopes rose slowly, for he saw in that slightly changing expression what he had desired.

The *doktor* smiled very slowly, a smile made hideous by those two tusk teeth sticking downward. He bowed, shot a glance at the big man in the shadow of the corner who had G-8 covered constantly with his Lugers.

"A thousand pardons, G-8. *Jawohl.* Of course I did not know. You are a brave man. You do not seem to fear death. I am indeed proud to have you for my prisoner."

"And you will comply with my last request before I am shot?"

The tusks showed plainly again as the *doktor* grinned.

"Should I refuse I would be unworthy of being called great," Krueger nodded. But there was only boasting and ego in that flat high voice. *"Jawohl.* I will tell you my plans before you are shot. It is a pleasure to tell someone else who is clever enough to understand the full meaning of my scheme."

G-8 grew slightly more tense. He measured the distance to the wide window above his head He moved as though to get closer to the *doktor* to listen more intently. And in so doing worked himself about slightly so that the *doktor* was between himself and the big German with the twin Luger guns.

"I listen, *Excellenz,*" G-8 said. "To hear the plan of the greatest scientist in the world before I die, hear it from his own lips, would be the highest ambition of my life."

The *Herr Doktor* Krueger swelled with pride.

"Listen," he hissed, "I shall tell you. Remember the story of the bats of the poison breath that came five hundred years ago to spread destruction upon the Rhone Valley, *Mein Herr?*"

G-8 hardly realized whether he himself caused his head to nod or whether it was the sudden shudder that passed through him that made it bob in response. *Doktor* Krueger didn't seem to notice. He was working up to a feverish heat as he talked on.

"I, *Herr Doktor* Krueger, have found that this story was true," he went on. "These great bats have lived in a giant cave in the Jura Mountains above the Rhone Valley for five hundred years. I have discovered them. They have been locked in the cave by a landslide which came five hundred years ago. They have grown to enormous size. *Ja.*"

G-8 broke into a laugh.

"How do you get those pipe dreams, *Herr Doktor?*" he asked in sudden derision. "Do you take it in the arm or sniff it?"

The tiny eyes of Krueger flamed suddenly until they glowed like coals of fire. He leaned forward and clutched G-8's arm.

"You do not believe me? I would take you there to show you that *Herr Doktor* Krueger does not lie. But the tunnel is not finished as yet."

"And what's this tunnel got to do with the bats?" G-8 hurled back at him.

"Got to do with it—*Gott im Himmel!*" *Doktor* Krueger was growing highly excited. "It is the connection between Germany and the cave of the bats where they have been growing to huge size for five hundred years, *ja.*"

G-8 nodded calmly, smiled.

THE BAT STAFFEL

"That's another thing I wanted to know. And I suppose you've got these bats trained so they'll go out when you turn them loose and kill every man, woman and child from the Rhone to Paris."

The great head of *Doktor* Krueger was nodding excitedly.

"Ja! Jawohl! Das ist richt. And we shall win the war for the *Vaterland.* Science will win the war, *nicht wahr!* But wait. Perhaps yet you do not believe. You are sentenced to die before a firing squad for being a spy. Perhaps this would be more to your liking. To die by the breath of the bat. Wait, I shall show you how quick, how easy it is. How complete."

DOKTOR **KRUEGER** turned quickly and strode toward the dark corner. G-8 stared after him. He wished that big German with the twin Lugers would leave, too. He wanted to stand upright. This kinked position of the crippled peasant was getting cramped. But he must hold that against a future plan. That plan must work.

But the great guard with his two guns did not leave the corner of the room. He simply moved aside a few inches so that Krueger could pass.

A half minute and Krueger's quick step sounded on the hard stone floor. He strode rapidly toward G-8. In his hands he carried a cylinder such as is used for holding highly compressed gasses, and a cage with a guinea pig inside.

He set the two on the table in the center of the room. G-8 moved closer. He tensed there. Something came to him from outside the old castle. A sound. A humming roar. He felt rather than saw *Doktor* Krueger turn and face him.

"*Das ist* my messenger getting off in an airplane with my plans for the tunnel," he explained. "Now you will look here, *bitte*. I turn on the gas for the guinea pig. Watch closely."

G-8 was watching closely. But his mind wasn't away from that racing airplane motor for one instant. Probably the *doktor* in his enthusiasm and assurance that G-8 was going to die had spoken the truth. The plans would soon be on their way for the completion of the tunnel to that mythical cave of the bats. The roar came from a Mercedes. G-8, with his uncanny sense of sound, was sure of that.

"Now I turn on the breath of the bat," Krueger was saying.

A slight hissing sound could be heard. G-8 stared. The nozzle of the tank was very close to the nose of the guinea pig. The animal seemed simply to suddenly drop. Drop in sleep. But then something else happened. Following the falling into that sleep came the twitching of muscles and next the weirdest thing G-8 had ever seen.

The body of the guinea pig began to shrink. It shrank to half its original size. Then to a quarter its size.

Herr Doktor Krueger was grinning with fiendish joy.

"*Ja.* See it work?" He was babbling and boasting for the sheer joy of making a hideous demonstration. It meant nothing that G-8 before him was about to die. He only seemed wrapped up in his discovery. A successful scientist at work. A fiend about to take command of the world at will.

"Look. After killing the animal or man the body is destroyed. You watch long enough and you shall see only a very small pile of dust left of the guinea pig. That will be all. *Jawohl!*"

THE BAT STAFFEL

G-8 was tense as a ramrod. Tense, but still bent in his crippled shape that he must hold until the proper moment, he heard everything that Krueger explained and more. He heard as well the roar of two Hisso motors, outside the castle but far away.

Apparently Krueger hadn't heard the sound of those motors as yet. He was babbling on about his discovery.

"I will command the world with these bats," he raved. "But now comes the time for you to die." He spoke with a businesslike air—as though he had suddenly remembered that he must call a certain phone number or take a pill at a given time—and he was late.

His small, feminine hands lifted the gas tank.

"Come," he said, "it is time."

G-8 shot a glance past Krueger to the big German with his Lugers. He was still there. This was something G-8 hadn't bargained for. He shot another glance at the high window.

"Come. It is time for you to die. This gas will be easier. Besides, I have wanted to try it on some human being. Now is my chance. Take a deep breath, *Mein Herr* G-8."

CHAPTER 2
THE BAT BREATH

ALL THIS time G-8 had remained in his stooped position like a peasant crippled and bent with age. The *Herr Doktor* Krueger was very close to him, but at the side now. He held the tank of gas close to his nose. The slim, pointed fingers of the *doktor's* right hand were on the valve that would release the gas.

G-8 felt the cold chill of tension prickle along his spine. Out of the corner of his eye he could still see the big German standing in the darkened corner of the room. Those Lugers looked ugly, ready for action. Krueger was not between G-8 and the German with the twin guns now.

There came a hissing sound from the tank.

Stsssss!

That seemed to touch G-8 off, to blast him into action. No longer was he stooped and bent. Instead he leaped erect. His face moved away from the nozzle of the tank.

Crack!

One Luger spat and then the other.

Crack!

But G-8 had moved in anticipation of that. The tiny, close-set eyes of the great *Doktor* Krueger suddenly bulged from their sockets. A cry escaped his parted lips.

"*Gott im himmel!*"

That was a prayer more than a curse.

G-8 had leaped aside as two bullets spat and whistled past him to land with a sodden sound against the stone wall behind. But G-8 had leaped toward the *Herr Doktor* Krueger and in leaping had grasped the little *doktor* by the shoulders and had flung him around before him, holding him between the German guard with the guns and himself.

"*Gott*, do not shoot, Hans," Krueger cried, "You will hit me."

The big fellow with his two Lugers was moving about the

THE BAT STAFFEL

far end of the room, trying to get a safe shot past the form of his master.

Almost instantly Krueger raised his left hand. That was the hand that held the tank of deadly gas. He raised his hand to hurl the tank from him. But G-8 was there a split second ahead of him.

The master Yankee spy shot his right across, grasped the small wrist of *Herr Doktor* Krueger, forced it down again.

The German guard came closer. He came now like an automaton, step by step. Creeping nearer and nearer toward G-8, who held the *doktor* always between himself and those two Lugers.

With his left hand, G-8 held the *doktor* by the scrawny throat. The *doktor* gasped for breath. Gasped and cursed as he wriggled helplessly in the steel clutches of the American spy.

In his right hand, G-8 held the small tank of deadly gas. His fingers moved along toward the nozzle while he had the tank itself in the palm of his hand. He raised the tank to hurl it.

"Get back or I'll let this tank go," he warned the German.

A gasped explosion came from the open mouth of the scientist.

"That will do no good," he choked. "You cannot warn Hans. He knows nothing except that he is to give me protection. He has no thoughts other than that. I, the great *Doktor* Krueger, have performed the operation. He is mine."

The fingers of G-8 tightened about the throat of his enemy. The words were cut off, diminished to a gurgling sound.

"Oh, yeah?" he snapped.

G·8 AND HIS BATTLE ACES

His fingers were unscrewing the valve at the end of the tank. He raised it again to throw.

Crack!

Flaming steel ripped through his sleeve, gashed the arm that held the tank of gas.

"No!" choked the *Herr Doktor* Krueger. "No, we all be killed. Do not open that—"

But already the gas was hissing from the nozzle of the tank.

Stssss! Then a whistling sound and the tank flipped through the air like a torpedo. G-8 aimed with the skill of a master.

THE BAT STAFFEL

Crack!

Another shot echoed through the room and steel slashed through the shoulder of his peasant's costume.

Crunch!

The tank sped and landed. The big German tried to duck it. He was far too sluggish. It caught him flush on the mouth. The hissing continued. He staggered backward, clutched at air.

Then it seemed that his legs folded up beneath him, and he was going down, down, with that tank lying near, making that deadly hissing sound.

IN THE tense second that followed, while G-8 watched and continued to hold the little struggling, cursing *doktor* by the throat, the same thing happened to the big German guard that he had witnessed in the guinea pig. The muscles of the guard pulsed for but an instant. Then the body grew rigid and began to grow smaller in size.

A low, angry growl escaped G-8's throat. With all his might he flung the little *doktor* at the shrinking heap of flesh on the floor and whirled toward the window.

From behind came the cry of terror that was inevitable.

G-8 leaped for the window. It was high above his head, but there was a wide ledge on the inside. He got hold, pulled himself upward, stood on the ledge for an instant and turned for a last look at the dwarfing German guard and the *doktor*.

The horror of the whole affair almost made him shudder. The guard was already smaller in size than the little *doktor*. The *doktor* had leaped to his feet. He was holding his nose and mouth with one hand, snatching at one of the Lugers on the floor with the other.

The *Herr Doktor* Krueger whirled with the Luger to face G-8 poised on the sill.

Crash!

That was G-8 plunging through the window, soaring out into space beyond.

Crack-crack-crack!

The Luger spat and leaped three times in the small hand of the *doktor*. Lead slashed after G-8 as he lunged through a shower of glass and began to fall.

Struggling, fighting, G-8 seemed hurtling down for a fall of close to a hundred feet, straight down the side of the great castle to the ground.

Tall trees came up at him like feathered swords. He made a grab for a large branch sticking out. Missed. Grasped for another.

Bam! He got hold of that limb, hung on, slipped. The jerk as his body slowed its fall nearly tore his arms out by the roots. He felt suddenly weak and sick. His whole body ached from the shock.

He heard shouts from within the castle. Whirled and stared up at the shattered window from which he had just leaped.

A figure was already framed in that window. A German who was taking aim with a rifle.

Instantly, G-8 let go his hold. He was falling down again through heavy, green-covered branches. Dropping toward another limb fifteen feet below.

Crack crack!

The rifle barked twice and steel whistled overhead.

Bam! His feet hit the limb. He stopped. Green foliage covered him from view of the window now. Another and another wild shot came from above. He would be down there somewhere, they knew. They were shooting at random.

Again he leaped. He reached another branch farther down. Down, down, bruised and cut and scared, he made his way like a crazy ape, leaping from branch to branch.

Other men were shooting at him from niches in the wall. He glanced down fearfully. Thankful no Germans had shown themselves on the ground beneath as yet. When that happened he was about done.

Then the last drop came. Straight down for nearly twenty feet. His feet hit the sloping earth of the side hill that dropped away from the old, half-ruined castle wall.

HIS LEGS crumpled under his weight as he landed. He picked himself up and dove for the cover of the undergrowth at the side. Running, plunging, falling, rolling, he tore down the side of the hill on which the castle was built.

He heard shouts from behind him. And while those put wings on his feet, the sound of two Hissos overhead made him thrill with joy and hope. Through the leaves of the trees he made out two Spads circling at a thousand feet.

He heard the booming of archie guns at the edge of the wood. Heard the rattle of ground machine guns as they spat flame and death up toward those two Yank planes.

On and on G-8 ran. He was panting, exhausted. He wondered about his own Spad that he had landed in the darkness last evening. He got his directions and headed for the field where he had left it, hidden except from the air.

Doubtless these two Spads pilots had seen the Spad from the air. Yes, that would be it. Even now the two Spads were circling about the spot where G-8's Spad was half-hidden.

The shouts from behind had died away. G-8 was getting away from his pursuers, losing them in the tangle of underbrush. He broke across a field, skirted the edge and raced on.

Far in the distance he could faintly hear the hum of that Mercedes engine that had roared while he was talking with the *Herr Doktor*. That Mercedes engine that was carrying the ship with the plans of the tunnel.

G-8 broke upon the field where his Spad was hidden. He saw dead Germans spattering the field. The two Spads were diving and zooming at other Germans who tried to cross the field toward the spot where his own Spad stood.

Tac-tac-tac!

THE BAT STAFFEL

As they dove, their Vickers guns spat flames and tracers. One of the two Spads swerved and headed for G-8.

Instantly the master spy leaped into the air. He danced about like a wild man, held up his hands. Pointed toward the spot where his Spad stood. Made flapping motions with his hands.

The rattle of Vickers guns died away from that one diving ship. The Spad lunged and roared past so close that G-8 could have reached out and touched one of the wings with his hand.

He tore off his hat, raced for his plane. The other Spad bore down upon him now, but Vickers guns did not spurt flame from the nose. A small, grinning face peered at him as the plane thundered down and up past him. A small hand waved.

G-8 reached his half-hidden plane. The other two Spads had banked and were storming down on the Germans, running across the other end of the field.

Vickers rattled. Germans fell. And G-8 snapped on his switch, leaped to the prop and pulled it through twice.

Brumm! The Hisso started with a roar. No time to wait for warming exercises now. G-8 was panting as he climbed into the cockpit. Slowly, fearfully, he pushed the gun ahead. The Hisso snorted, picked up, snorted again.

He kicked the plane out of its hiding place and turned into the wind—directly into the faces of those running falling, dying Germans.

The Hisso was sluggish. Men before him took careful aim and fired upward. But the rudder bar see-sawed and the Spad bucked and leaped and twisted in a crazy course.

It grew lighter and climbed steadily. Holes appeared in wing covering and the turtle back. Appeared as though by magic. But death was poking those holes and no magician.

Higher and higher. G-8 skimmed the tree tops and turned toward the southeast. Far in the distance he could make out a tiny speck on the horizon. That would likely be the plane that carried the plans. At that distance he could make the plane out as an Albatros. He ought to be able to gain on it with a Spad.

He whirled in his seat, waved his arm to the pilots of the other two Spads to follow. They both banked, swung round and roared after him.

With G-8 at point and the other two planes forming the Vee formation, they thundered after the Albatros.

CHAPTER 3
HELL ISLAND

G-8 TURNED in his seat and surveyed the two companions of his new acquaintance. Master pilots, those two. He could tell that by the way they handled their planes, by the way they had put on that fight to keep the Germans away from his Spad to give him time to get it started and take the air. Master battle birds, those two.

Vaguely, he wondered who they were. He made out numbers on their ships. There was the Spad with the little fellow with the grinning face. That Spad was number thirteen.

The pilot of the other ship was larger, much larger than the pilot of Spad number 13. All G-8 could see of his face was the jaw. That seemed sufficient. The jaw was square and looked hard

THE BAT STAFFEL

as rock. His shoulders protruded from the cockpit and cramped the padding on the side. And the number of the ship that the great bull-necked, square-jawed, broad-shouldered pilot flew was 7.

As G-8 hurled on in pursuit of the Albatros he smiled to himself at the idea. Two pilots. One small and of apparently clever mind. A little chap who made up for his lack of strength by his brain. And he defied luck and superstition by having the number 13.

The other, the big, two-fisted brute of a man. He had a ready grin too and a nonchalant wave. But the lucky number, 7, told the story. He had superstitions. He trusted in luck. Perhaps his apparent great strength had taken away a little of his brain power.

Interesting combination, G-8 thought to himself. Two chaps worth knowing. What one couldn't think of in a jam the other would. He wondered if they were friends. Glanced again at their ships and squadron insignia. No, they didn't belong to the same outfit. Funny that, both flying out here together and from two different squadrons.

Then, out of the corner of G-8's eye he caught sight of something else. He had been watching the smaller pilot of the two. He suddenly saw the slight chap whirl in his seat as though by sudden premonition of danger.

Almost the same instant, G-8 felt that danger. His eyes shifted upward and behind. Up toward a cloud that hung white and fluffy in the glistening sunlight.

Fokkers were there. A flight of seven had suddenly tipped

over the edge of the cloud and were storming down on the three Spads.

G-8 whirled and stared ahead. He and his two new sky comrades had gained on the Albatros. And in gaining, they had gone farther and farther over into that part of Germany that lies north of Switzerland.

From behind came the Fokkers. They were at least a mile away. But they had the advantage of higher altitude. They were already diving with the additional speed that their great height would give them. Their Mercedes were churning and whining in a fiendish chant of hate.

G-8 turned. Both the other pilots seemed to be watching him for a sign. It was as though by unanimous consent G-8 had been placed in command of the flight of three.

His brain was working rapidly. They must never lose sight of that Albatros with the plans. But a dogfight was inevitable. The Fokkers would be upon them before they could catch up with the racing Albatros.

He turned to motion. His hand went up in a sign to wait, then slowly it described a complete circle. A loop.

He watched eagerly to see if he was understood. Two heads nodded. The big Yank, the boy in number 7, held his hand still for a moment and then flipped it over. The little chap in Spad number 13 simply grinned and nodded.

G-8 glanced at the Fokkers behind. They were coming, coming. He was sure they were too far away to see or interpret his sign to the other two.

The three Spads held their course for the fleeing Albatros.

THE BAT STAFFEL

Not until G-8 heard the warming burst of Spandaus guns did he turn again. Then he twisted sharply about as though taken by surprise.

He gaped at the diving Fokkers. Held himself rigid. His signal must come just at the right time. He could see that both other pilots were for some reason trusting him implicitly. They hadn't even glanced back when the warning burst had rattled from the fourteen enemy guns.

NEARER AND nearer came the Fokkers. G-8 sat twisted round in his seat and watched with a strained expression on his still made-up face.

Fokkers within range now. They might open fire at any moment. The time had come for the maneuver.

Now!

Like a great battering ram, being thrust into the air and brought down once more instantly, the fist of G-8 shot upward and down. The signal for the maneuver.

Three Hisso's snarled as noses dropped for a split second. Then wings and wire and wood and steel groaned as the three Spads, still in perfect formation, looped high in the air.

Tac-tac-tac!

Spandaus lead spat just as they leaped. Yellow German tracer ribbons fluffed beneath the snarling Spads.

Up, and up they roared. On their backs now. Moving so fast they could scarcely be followed with the untrained eye.

Fokker pilots, taken almost entirely off their guard, tried to follow. The leader gave it up, ordered his pilots to straighten their course once more, to lessen danger of collision in the air with each other.

Before it could be fully realized, the three Spads had finished their loops. The Fokkers had shot on beneath them. And now the three Spads were on the tails of seven Fokker planes.

G-8 glared across his sights. His hand pressed the trigger button. White tracers slithered from his twin Vickers guns as they bucked and snarled.

The lead Fokker seemed to stub its toe—or would it be the landing gear? At any rate it started on a jerky outside loop, motor foremost. Down, down and down. But it never once came out of that plunge for the earth.

G-8 didn't wait to see that ship go down beyond the line of his sights. The minute he had pressed his trigger button his skill and experience told him that Jerry was doomed.

A tinge of red to the right caught the corner of his eye, told him that another Fokker was going down. Or was it a Fokker? Yes. For an instant Spad 13 had been so close to the doomed Fokker he couldn't be sure.

G-8 was snarling on the tail of another Jerry with blazing guns when he felt the drum of steel on his tail group. He whirled. Held his fire long enough to see a second Jerry go down before his Vickers. Then he yanked and kicked controls.

Tac-tac-tac!

Above the bark of Spandau guns came the rip and rattle of other Vickers. Spad number 7 was snarling down on the tail of the Fokker that had cut loose and dived on the tail of G-8. The pilot of Spad 7 loomed large in the cockpit.

THE BAT STAFFEL

G-8 turned as he half-rolled and stared back. Even as he sent his Spad into a convulsion he watched that face with the square, rock-like jaw. A perfect fighting face. Cold, and yet flaming eyes, were those of the pilot of Spad 7 as they glared across the sights.

The Fokker tried valiantly to follow the maneuver of G-8. But few, if any German pilots, ever successfully followed a move of the master Yank spy.

Tac-tac-tac!

That was a short burst from the guns of Spad 7. But it was sufficient—and more. The Jerry pilot slumped in his seat. His mouth drew to one side. The ship began to plunge. As it burst into flame, the Jerry pulled himself up in the cockpit with an effort, slipped over the side and tumbled out of the blazing plane.

Falling to his death, he waved a last gallant salute to his comrades and the pilot who had sent him to his doom.

G-8 gulped. He saw the lips of the big Yank move as though in a curse. Then he knew it must have been a prayer instead, because the pilot of Spad 7 jerked his goggles upward for an instant and slapped at his watery eyes with a grease-smeared palm.

THE WORLD had seemed to stop for one, two seconds for that bit of melodrama from life. But only for that short time did it stop. Then the pilot of Spad 13 was diving and leaping and snapping at two Fokkers like a rat terrier at a vermin picnic.

Another Fokker went down before his guns. G-8 was rolling away from a Fokker that harried his tail. He turned the trick,

dove on that Fokker and sent him down with a disabled Mercedes engine.

Only one Fokker remained in the sky. And that Jerry plane was already on the run for home. The two Spads drew nearer to G-8. The small pilot with that likable, perpetual grin and the big Yank with his square, rock-like jaw looked at G-8 now. They waited as they flew a bit behind with expressions on their faces that seemed to ask of their new leader:

THE BAT STAFFEL

G-8 glared across his sights; his hand pressed the trigger button.

"What next?"

G-8 pointed at once toward the Albatros. Hardly three minutes had elapsed since the dogfight began. But this was valuable time lost in the pursuit of the fleeing messenger plane.

G-8 glanced toward the south now, spotted it far away. It was a mere speck on the horizon. And beyond it rose in bold, white relief the jagged peaks of the Alps with their eternal crowns of snow. He jammed the throttle to full ahead and roared on. Spads thirteen and seven hugged in close on either side. They roared on together.

Minutes ticked by. At times they seemed to be gaining. At others, they hardly seemed to get nearer that fleeing ship.

But they were gaining. Five minutes, ten minutes, then fifteen—and they had drawn near enough to the Albatros to make out the pilot's head turning to see them in pursuit.

They were flying along the upper valley of the Rhine where it winds its way between Germany and Switzerland on toward France.

Nearer and nearer they came, gaining, gaining. They could see the white of the pilot's face.

Suddenly the Albatros dropped toward an island that was distinguished by a small clearing in the center. The island was rough and rocky on one side. The level place looked smooth and fit for landing. Toward this the pilot was diving. G-8 dropped his nose in pursuit. The others did the same. After a moment the Yank spy whirled, pointed to his comrades and then into the air. Next he pointed to himself and down. The others nodded. They understood the sign language.

THE BAT STAFFEL

They would stay in the air on watch. G-8, on the other hand, would land and capture the Jerry pilot, the *offizier* who had the long envelope with the plans for the tunnel that was to be a means of spreading death over all of France, perhaps over the world, if the fiend, *Herr Doktor* Krueger, was successful.

The Albatros was going down in an easy glide. Just to make sure, G-8 ranged down beside it and opened fire, slashing the right wing of the German ship with his Vickers lead.

The pilot turned instantly, held up both hands for the briefest moment, then turned to his landing once more. He was signifying his surrender.

Suddenly, G-8 sat bolt upright in his cockpit. Something was wrong. The Jerry pilot was overshooting the field. He was going to end his roll in that great, overhanging clump of trees that formed one boundary. Down at that end where the high cliff of rocks ran to the river's edge.

G-8 tried to shout in warning. But already the engine of the Albatros had died. Already the wheels were rolling. The plane was racing for that clump of green ahead.

G-8 kicked over and stormed down for a quick landing. He came in short, his wheels touched and rolled.

But he seemed to be too late. The Albatros disappeared suddenly into the mass of trees. And from that green bower came a crackling, crashing sound. Then smoke and, a split second later, flame.

The ship had crashed. It was burning. Those plans would be burned.

Wildly, G-8 leaped from his cockpit, lit running and raced toward the roaring inferno.

CHAPTER 4
THE VANISHED ACE

HEAT SCORCHED his face as he tore through the leafy branches and broke upon the burning wreckage of the Albatros. He stood appalled for the moment, trying to decide whether it was too late to attempt to save the pilot and his valuable envelope.

In that moment of hesitation he noticed something that caused his eyes to bulge. Sheets of flame had been sweeping over the ship, shutting the entire cockpit from view. Now, with startling abruptness, the cockpit was visible as the fire swept momentarily to another part of the wreck.

The cockpit was empty!

G-8 gasped—puzzled. He ran around to the front where he could get a better look. There was no doubt. The cockpit of the Albatros was empty. No living or dead man was in it. Only the empty, blazing seat was there. And in that glance, G-8 glimpsed something else. The safety belt had not torn loose. It was unbuckled. Had been unbuckled, apparently, by the Jerry pilot.

Nothing seemed to move on that island in the upper Rhine. Except for the crackling of the flames that were dying out for want of fuel, all was still. To be sure, the two Spads thundered overhead, but the island was still. Nothing moved.

G-8 ran to the other side of the plane.

THE BAT STAFFEL

"That Heinie *Kapitan* didn't look like any fool," he said half aloud. "Probably he unbuckled his belt so the plane would throw him clear when it tangled up with the trees. Ought to find him lying around somewhere in front of the ship. He's not burned, that's one good thing. Ought to have that envelope on him."

The flames were dying out. G-8 searched about in the brush, but found nothing.

It began to dawn upon him that there was something strange here. A man didn't vanish from a crashed plane and disappear on a small island without leaving a trace of where he had gone.

One of the Spads was coming in to land. G-8 watched it with a frown. The Spad touched and rolled. A small, alert chap leaped from the cockpit like a monkey and ran toward G-8 and the burning plane.

The other Spad remained aloft, circling low above their heads. The small, keen-eyed pilot grinned as he came up.

"If you're looking for the guy that was flying this Albatros, better start hunting among those rocks," he called. As he spoke he pointed to the mass of jagged rocks that formed the north end of the island.

G-8 whirled and stared. His frown became more troubled.

"I don't get you," he said.

"Didn't think you would. I'm used to disappearing acts. I spotted this bird from the air when he crashed his plane. I couldn't see him climb out or set fire to it, but I saw him dive out of the trees here and go among those rocks up ahead. Then I lost him."

Already G-8 had spun around and was making for the mass

of rocks beyond. They were great boulders, some as large as a house, others only the size of a small car. They were tumbled in a mad confusion, apparently by nature. Here and there great chinks opened into winding chasms.

G-8 plunged down one of these. His feet slipped. He came up with a thud against a great blank wall of stone, eight or ten feet below the surface of the ground.

Scrambling, clawing, he managed to get back. The young pilot with the grin, who flew Spad number 13, watched him intently, helping him out finally when he nearly reached the top.

Baffled, G-8 mounted to the highest boulder and surveyed the mass from his perch. Slowly he shook his head.

"Funny," he mused, "but I'll gamble that bird is around somewhere. He's hiding in one of these holes."

G-8 heard the little pilot of 13 laugh just below him.

"Sure," chuckled the other, "but find the hole. That's the trick."

G-8 leaped from his perch and began a careful investigation. It seemed every crevasse between the boulders left a hole large enough for a man to crawl through. There seemed to be a hundred odd holes—perhaps more.

Suddenly, G-8 stood up, listened. Spad number 7 roared closer. G-8 turned his eyes toward the north. He tensed for an instant. Then like a tight spring suddenly released, he lunged down off the heap of stone and raced for his ship.

The pilot of Spad 13 was close behind. The two gained their ships about the same time. Spad number 7 roared down in a

THE BAT STAFFEL

dive over their heads. The big square-jawed pilot shouted a warning above the thunder of his Hisso.

"Jerry flight comin'. Let's go!"

G-8 waved as his motor caught. The little pilot of Spad 13 ran through with his prop.

Two Spads were hurling into the air at the same time. Spad 13 with its lighter pilot got off first. G-8 was close behind. As he turned he stared into the north at the oncoming enemy planes.

They were making for that lone island in the Rhine. It was as though that pilot of the Albatros, the *Kapitan,* had sent out a message for help by wireless.

The idea stuck in G-8's mind. Perhaps he had. No telling what this island held, those rocks with their many niches. They might lead to anything. Might lead to a cave of some kind even under the Rhine. That thought caused him to sit up a little straighter in his seat.

"Might be," he mused. "This island is just about where the Rhine River runs along the Swiss-Franco-German border."

He turned his attention from the rocks at the end of the island. He had been staring down at those while he made a circle over them. To the north a flight of five Pfalz planes droned at them. They had apparently just left some field not so far away because they were climbing rapidly as they came.

G-8 faced the other two pilots. They stood at either side of him, waiting, ready. There seemed to be a mutual understanding between them, although none knew the name of another. And

G-8 still wore the clothing of a peasant and had the make-up on his face of an aged man with a twisted nose.

Five Pfalz stormed down upon them with rattling guns. They were still at long range. G-8 seemed to hesitate. Duty insisted that he return to headquarters as soon as possible. Instinct demanded that he stay and fight.

He stayed, shot his fist into the air for a sign of combat. He got a grin as a mark of okay from each of the other pilots. They kicked their Spads round and hurled into the mass of Pfalz.

Flying a leaping, bucking course, G-8 took the Jerry leader on for a private battle. Up and up and up they maneuvered. Then abruptly, G-8 changed his movements and plunged on the tail of his surprised opponent.

He didn't wait to see the leader of that Pfalz flight crash in the waters of the Rhine. G-8 broke loose and lunged at another. Spad 13 and its keen little pilot was darting about as usual. There was something fascinating about the way that youngster fought in the air. He hardly flew a straight course for more than ten feet. He was constantly on the alert, jabbing in, darting away. His guns were speaking in short effective bursts.

A Jerry crate went down before the guns of Spad 7 and the big square-jawed pilot. He fought like a bulldog. Once he got on the tail of an E.A. There was no shaking him off until that Jerry crate had folded up and left for parts unknown.

G-8 was fighting his usually masterful battle of the air. Each of the Yanks had one Pfalz apiece. The two remaining enemy ships turned to flee, then suddenly seemed to take heart. They banked and came back to fight.

THE BAT STAFFEL

G-8 stared past them. A black cloud of enemy aircraft was storming up from the north. He watched it with a frown for half a minute. He was higher than the rest of the ships now. Spad 13 and the little pilot were sending down another Pfalz. The last had turned back again and was racing now for home.

For a long moment, G-8 studied that mass of enemy ships coming toward them. There were Fokkers and Pfalz and Albatrosses. Some fifty of them perhaps. Fokkers were leading. Queer, that sudden massing of ships to drive three Spads out of the sky.

He hesitated only a moment longer; then he signaled for a hurried flight toward their own lines.

As they turned, the enemy *jagdstaffel* gained on them. Fokkers left the others behind slowly and crept up on the three Spads.

G-8 stared back at the two pilots with him. He got their okay again in their grins above their cockpit cowlings. That lessened his feeling of guilt at running, even from a number of ships like this. It always went against the grain when G-8 had to back up in his course. But there were times when it was better to back away gracefully. He was doing it now.

The rugged Vosges Mountains pointed their fingers up at them as they thundered above. Giant fingers, they seemed, ready to clutch these three frail Spads and crush them at a stroke.

The distance between the leading Fokkers and the three Spads remained the same. Finally the enemy ships turned back and became mere specks in the northern horizon.

Past Nancy and Toul and then to Colombey Les Belles the

three Spads flew together. At the latter airdrome, Spad 7 pulled alongside and pointed down.

G-8 frowned, then he shook his head.

The grin was gone from the face of the big square-jawed pilot of Spad number 7. He glared at G-8, pointed down again.

Again G-8 shook his head.

He turned his head, caught sight of the alert little pilot of Spad 13 pulling along on the other side of him.

The smaller pilot was also pointing down. He seemed very much in earnest. The thought suddenly struck G-8 humorously. He laughed outright as he shook his head.

At that instant Spad 7 leaped into the air and the next second G-8 found Spad 7 on his tail. White tracers slashed through a right wing but a safe distance from the cockpit.

G-8 continued to smile. Spad number 13 had pulled a quick half loop and roll. Vickers guns snarled from its nose. G-8 was caught in the cross-fire. But neither of the Spads was shooting dangerously close.

"These two," he smiled, "are either over curious, or very determined about their duty. I'd probably do the same thing if I saw a bird come out with a phony make-up and dressed as a peasant and then fly away in a Spad and do a lot of tricks with it. I'd help as much as I could, but when we got back home I'd want to know what it was all about." He laughed again. "But there isn't time now. Got to get to headquarters. We'll have some fun though. Here goes!"

At the touch of the expert hand of G-8, the Spad leaped in a sudden zoom. But that was only the start. Round and round

THE BAT STAFFEL

the ship rolled. It looped, it bucked, it stalled. And all of the time the two other Spads tried desperately to follow. Tried, struggled and failed in their futile attempt.

Then, when it seemed that G-8 and his flashing Spad were about to break away and run for it, the Spad turned and hurled back. Guns blazed.

Tail groups of both the other two planes were sieved with slugs from the cavorting Spad that the master spy flew. And when both the pilot of Spad 13 and the pilot of Spad 7 were about to go insane in their efforts to shake him from their tails, G-8 leaped away.

He held up his hand as he roared away. Held it up, brought the thumb to his nose, grinned and turned toward Paris.

CHAPTER 5
G-8, SPECIAL AGENT

THE SPAD circled over Le Bourget Field and prepared to land. Mechanics recognized the plane, ran at once to help. G-8 climbed from the cockpit. Walking hurriedly to the nearest hangar, he entered by a small door on the side.

At once a middle-aged man snapped to attention. He bowed and smiled with the pleased air of an old dog rejoicing to see its master.

"I'm delighted to see you back so soon, sir."

G-8 laughed. He slapped the older man on the narrow back. "And believe me, Battle, I'm glad to be back. Looked as though I wouldn't make it for a while, but as usual my luck came through to help."

G-8 stretched out in a long, reclining chair. The man servant called Battle went at once to work on the spy's face. He dabbed at the make-up first removing the twisted nose. He picked cautiously. For to touch that make-up was to believe that it was the genuine face of G-8. And while the man servant worked, he talked.

"Blessed if that isn't like you, sir," he said. "Always giving credit to either luck or the devil, sir, for what you come through, and everybody sayin', sir, beggin' you pardon, that you're the cleverest spy any country has ever had, sir."

G-8 laughed, then winced a little as the make-up pulled hair and skin in the process of being taken off.

"Quit your bragging and make it snappy, Battle…. I've got to high tail it to Paris headquarters as soon as I can. Got a lot of dates with some bats."

"Bats, sir?" inquired Battle. "Don't tell me, sir, you're going in for church steeple climbing. I've heard of bats in the belfry, sir. I recall when I was a lad I—"

"Ouch!" sputtered G-8, sitting upright. He felt of his face. Battle gave him a hurt look.

"I was thinking of the bats, sir."

"Forget it," G-8 winced. "Maybe I shouldn't have mentioned it. I guess I can wash the rest of it off."

He plunged his head into a bucket of soapy water, and emerged presently with his face wrapped in a towel. After a vigorous scrubbing and drying he looked in a mirror. He smiled.

THE BAT STAFFEL

THE PEASANT

"Well, Battle, at least the Heinie's have never seen G-8 to know who he is. That's something. Not to have anyone in a country know who you are, or what you really look like, eh, Battle?"

"Quite right, sir," bowed Battle. "My master, the great actor, Harden, whom I worked for before I came with you, sir, used to say that my make-ups were so clever that for—"

"—twenty years he hadn't really known just what he did look like himself in the naked flesh, sir," G-8 finished with a chuckle. "Some day we'll put that an a phonograph record to save you the trouble, Battle."

While he talked he slipped into the newly-pressed

G-8 THE SPECIAL MESSENGER

43

uniform of a captain of the American Air Service. That was his own uniform. G-8 was a spy, but his proudest possession was that captain's uniform with the wings and bars he had earned. Swiftly he buckled on his Sam Brown belt and turned.

"Going to Paris and headquarters, Battle." He slapped his make-up chief and man servant affectionately on the shoulder. "If Mr. Kaiser calls up while I'm out, take the message and tell him to hold everything until I get back."

"Kaiser, Kaiser, sir," puzzled Battle. "Somehow I don't recall a Mr. Kaiser among your friends, sir."

G-8 turned at the door.

"You wouldn't," he called back. "He's a bird I almost met over in Germany."

The door slammed. G-8 left, chuckling.

He seemed vastly different as he took his seat in a low, fast roadster and whirled out of the hangar. He was not tall and not short either. A young man of medium build. Rather good-looking but no collar ad. He had broad shoulders and an easy rolling motion when he walked or moved that gave hint of having every muscle at his instant command.

But those steel-gray eyes were the outstanding thing about this master spy. They held one by a sort of magnetism even while in casual conversation. They were commanding eyes.

THE CAR drew swiftly to a stop before a great building of Paris. A guard moved forward to take command of it as G-8 stepped to the curb. A moment later G-8 was being ushered without the slightest hesitation or question into the office of the high command of the Secret Service in France.

THE BAT STAFFEL

Another high-ranking officer was present. G-8 paused and saluted respectfully.

"I'm sorry," he said. "I didn't know I was breaking in on a conference."

G-8 blinked for an instant. He had counted those stars wrong on the shoulder straps of the high officer. Five stars were there. The great general smiled.

"You're not interrupting at all, G-8," he said. "In fact we were just talking about you and your excellent work. I take it you have important news again?"

G-8 nodded.

"Most important," he said. "Although I'm afraid I'll have to admit that I've partially failed so far."

"Failed?" frowned the great general.

"Well, that is, to some extent. I'll come to that later. You see, sir, I have heard rumors about a certain *Herr Doktor* Krueger who is a master scientist. I met him today."

"You—met Krueger?" That came from the astonished lips of both the general and the head of the Secret Service at the same instant.

"There wasn't any other way out of it," G-8 half apologized.

"But good heavens, man!" exploded the general. "We can't have you walking right into the jaws of death like that. Why, G-8, you're the most valuable man in the Secret Service. You can't afford to take chances like that."

G-8 laughed.

"It wasn't so much of a chance, not the way it worked out," he said. "You see I went over last evening disguised as a peasant, an old duck bent with age. I managed to sneak into Freiburg Castle. But I found that the *Herr Doktor's* offices and quarters were too heavily guarded to get by with mere nerve—that way, at least. So I permitted myself to be taken prisoner, and when they grilled me after my capture I admitted that I was a spy. But I wouldn't tell them who I was. I insisted on seeing the *Herr Doktor* Krueger before I would tell them."

The general groaned. G-8 laughed.

"That didn't work. They sentenced me to be shot an hour after dawn. But while I was hanging around the castle late last evening I overheard just what I was waiting for. I got the tip of a devilish plan on the part of this demon *Doktor* Krueger. I overheard something about a tunnel—through Switzerland. I put together all the pieces of things I had heard. It didn't make much of a story without the rest of the connecting links. So I let the *offizier* in charge of me know that I knew there was a master much higher than he was. And I let him know that I knew about a tunnel through Switzerland."

"And they took you to this fiend, Krueger?" the head of the Secret Service demanded.

"And how!" laughed G-8. "That was exactly what I wanted. It gave me a chance to work on the *Doktor's* vanity. Most great geniuses are egotists in one form or another. They love to boast about what they have done. So I simply told the *Herr Doktor* Krueger who I was and let him think that I considered him the possessor of the cleverest brain in the world. From then on there was no holding him. He told me everything. Of course he told me those things believing I was about to die and it wouldn't matter."

The general and the head of the Secret Service took long breaths, sighed deeply and glanced significantly at each other. **G-8 TOLD** what he had learned. Repeated the story of the bats sealed up in their mammoth cave for five hundred years, of their deadly breath. He smiled.

"Of course that yarn about the bats being sealed up in that cave for five hundred years is pretty phony," he said. "I can't swallow that. But that bat's breath—or whatever it is—sure is potent stuff. I saw it work—twice."

The eyes of the two high officials were bulging from their sockets.

"It's the most damnable stuff I've ever seen," G-8 went on. "Kills instantly. Doesn't leave anything after it finishes but a little heap of ashes. When I escaped from the *Herr Doktor's* rooms in the Freiburg Castle I hot-footed it—or rather hot-planed it—after another plane. Krueger had sent the plans for the completion of the tunnel with a *Kapitan,* the one who had had charge of me."

He told of the fight and the chase. Of the mysterious disappearance of that *offizier* after the plane had burned.

"While this story about the bats may be a fairy tale," G-8 went on, "that gas is real. Think what it means if it is loosed over France. Over the world. That fiend, Krueger, could rule the world with that stuff."

The general shuddered.

The head of the Secret Service in France gaped.

The two exchanged baffled glances.

"You—you tried to stop those plans from reaching their destination?" the general asked. "And you failed?"

"That's what I meant by failure," G-8 admitted. "But the fact that they probably reached their destination doesn't matter so much. It's the fact that I didn't get the plans. That I lost the chance to get them."

"You mean," asked the Secret Service head, "that with those plans you would have been able to learn perhaps the location of this supposed cave over in the Rhone Valley somewhere or wherever it is supposed to be."

"Right," said G-8. "You see I have a hunch that there is a passage from that island in the Rhine. A passage that will lead

THE BAT STAFFEL

to the tunnel through Switzerland. That German *offizier* who carried the plans and crashed the Albatros dove into that right opening in the rocks. It probably connected with the main tunnel. From there he sent the wireless that brought half the ships of Germany to kill us before we could get back with the information we had."

The two high officials exchanged worried, anxious glances. For a long moment neither spoke. The great general turned slowly, reluctantly, as though he feared putting the next question.

"Have you any plans for stopping this hideous scheme?" he asked in a voice that was shaken with anxiety.

G-8 nodded.

"Yes, sir," he answered, "But I'll need a little help, perhaps, although I'm not sure. I might be able to work it alone."

The general turned to the Secret Service head.

"You remember what we were discussing when G-8 entered?"

"Of course," came the answer.

"And you are in agreement with my suggestion?"

"Entirely, general."

"Very well, then."

With great dignity the commanding general of the Yanks turned and faced G-8.

"G-8," he said, "you are very young. Very young for so much responsibility. However, I—we—have great confidence in you and your ability. Everyone has confidence in you. Few men have ever looked upon your face and known it as the face of G-8, the master spy. But there isn't a doughboy in the trenches or a cook in a mess shack or a mule skinner or an officer who hasn't heard of you, who doesn't have complete confidence in you."

G-8 shifted nervously. He grinned sheepishly. The pink of embarrassment was creeping into his cheeks.

"General," he said, "if you wouldn't mind cutting the eulogy part of this obituary short and go into the straight sermon I'd be mighty grateful to you. My face is getting redder all the time. That's nice stuff you're saying, but just what had you planned to tell me—I mean that really matters?"

The great general broke into a laugh.

"That's like you, G-8," he chuckled. "I'll come to the point at once. Your chief here and I were just talking about you when you came in. There was some slight hesitation, but this last discovery of yours, I believe, makes this move on our part imperative."

The general drew himself up importantly.

"We have decided to make you a special agent of the spy system of America. A special independent system. It will be your own. No one will take command over you. You may choose any assistants you wish. You may take matters entirely in your own hands. You will answer to no one but us, and that will be at your discretion. Your first job will be to stop this deadly plan of the fiend, Krueger. From then on you will receive various assignments. Is that satisfactory to you?"

Slowly, deliberately, G-8 nodded.

"Entirely, sir," he answered. "And may I say no man could be more highly honored than by this trust. Count on me to do my best, general."

THE BAT STAFFEL

The great general held out his hand.

"God bless you, son, and good luck," he said fervently.

"Thank you, sir," G-8 answered.

He turned then and strode from the office.

THE POWERFUL roadster sped back to Le Bourget field and whirled into the hangar. G-8 leaped from the seat and bolted into his private quarters. He grinned, slapped Battle on the back.

"My friend, Kaiser, called up yet?" he kidded.

"Ah—er—no, sir. No one has called, sir."

G-8 stepped to a little portable phonograph. A record was in place. He placed the needle on it and gave the disc a whirl. A jazz tune squawked from the sound box. "Raggin' the Scale" seemed to galvanize the whole room into action.

G-8 paced the floor and puffed at a cigarette. He lighted a fresh one from the old, drew out maps, studied them. Battle cut in on his thought—as usual.

"Speaking of bats, sir," he said, "beggin' your pardon, sir, I remember as a boy my grandmother used to say that the blasted creatures were horrible if they got in the hair."

G-8 smiled.

"No doubt," he said absently and went on with his pacing. He drew plans on paper, snatched the phone and called the main library in Paris.

"Deliver to G-8 at Le Bourget all books pertaining to caves in the Jura Mountains." He hung up again.

Battle cut in with a laugh.

"Begging your pardon, sir, I was just thinking of the Kaiser gentleman you mentioned a bit ago, sir. Imagine my never once thinkin' you were jokin', sir. Why, no doubt you had in mind Kaiser Wilhelm of Germany, what? Imagine, sir."

"Imagine," grinned G-8. "Bats in the belfry, eh, Battle?"

G-8 didn't wait for a reply. He picked the phone from his desk again and shot an order into the mouthpiece.

"Get me the commandant of the field at Colombey Les Belles."

A wait of a few minutes, which was fast action for war-time France. But G-8 was used to fast action. A voice came back over the wire. An orderly inquired who wanted to speak to the high command of the great Yank airdrome.

The master spy simply said, "G-8."

Hardly had those magic words left his lips than an authoritative voice sounded over the wire.

"Seeking information about two of your men, colonel," G-8 said quickly. "One is in squadron 94. A small chap who flies Spad number 13. The other is in squadron 256, also stationed at your field. I'll hold the wire, sir. I want to know their names and whether they understand German. Is that clear?"

It was. G-8 had to wait only a few minutes to receive the information he requested.

After he had hung up, Battle hovered about him with a puzzled expression.

"But, sir, if I may be so bold, sir, I can't see what bats in the belfry might have to do with the present ruler of Germany, no matter how much one might dislike him, sir."

G-8 laughed.

THE BAT STAFFEL

"Consider it never said, Battle," he chuckled. "Now get busy packing. We're moving very shortly. Going for a vacation over near Switzerland, Battle."

CHAPTER 6
BATTLE ACES

AT THE very moment that G-8 called the colonel in command of the airdrome at Colombey Les Belles regarding the pilots of Spads 7 and 13, the pilot of Spad 13 was busily engaged in a strange sort of ceremony.

He was small, this pilot of Spad 13. Weston was his name. Everyone on the Front had heard of "Nippy" Weston, the youngster who mixed knocking Germans out of the air with certain feats of magic in his off times.

Nippy Weston, the ace. Nippy Weston, the magician. The kid who was able to grin at all things. Life to Nippy Weston seemed just one great illusion—like his tricks. Something to laugh at and through.

At the very moment that G-8 spoke to the colonel, Nippy was phoning a pal. They had been old friends, these two. Strange friends. The one small and fast as lightning. The other big and powerful.

"Listen, Bull," Nippy was saying. "Come on over to my quarters. Got something to show you. Yeah. Boy, you'll go nuts when you see it." He chuckled under his breath. "That-a-boy. Make it snappy."

He slammed the receiver on the hook and whirled to make

strange movements. He pulled down the window shades, plunging the room into total darkness.

Then, hurriedly, he arranged strips of cheese cloth that glowed in the darkness. Taking a piece of light spring wire, he twisted and bent it. He moved rapidly about the dark room with perfect ease and quiet.

When, a moment later, the door burst open and the great form of Bull Martin, pilot of Spad number 7, was framed in the opening for a moment, Nippy Weston was ready.

A low moaning sound came from every wall of the room. Bull Martin had stepped inside. Now he stopped short and blinked at the darkness.

"Hey," he sputtered with the first trace of nervousness, "What goes on?"

"*Whooooo!*" Again that wailing sound.

Then, apparently from right out of the opposite wall, drifted a weird white shapeless thing that fluttered and expanded as it floated toward the astonished newcomer.

A hoarse, nervous laugh came from Bull's mouth. And at the same time he turned. He seemed unable to control himself. He was big and strong and no fool. But something about that wailing sound, and the drifting white floating toward him unnerved him.

He whirled, reached out with powerful hands and tried to catch the door.

Bam! The door slammed shut before he could touch it. His hands reached the knob and he yanked. The knob came off in his fists. The door remained closed. The thing of white contin-

THE BAT STAFFEL

ued to drift toward him, and the wailing sound increased to almost a scream.

"Hey, you little squirt," Bull Martin growled in a shaky voice. "Cut it out. I know it's only you, but it's too real a show." He shivered. "Specially after I've just killed two or three Heinies this morning. What's the idea?"

The moaning ceased. The white apparition disappeared. Someone was laughing. Nippy Weston was laughing. The lights flashed on.

Nippy stood grinning in the middle of the room. Bull Martin moved with surprising speed for a man of his size and strength. Nippy ducked under his arm and came up on the other side.

But Bull's lunges and weight carried him to victory in that friendly scuffle. He cornered Nippy in the small room and was leaning over him, pretending to choke him, when a knock sounded on the door.

Instant silence fell. Bull got up noiselessly. Nippy whispered in his ear.

"That's my latest trick. Just worked it out. Here's another sucker at the door. We'll work it together. Hide behind the desk and start moaning when the door opens. I'll work the rest."

"Okay!" hissed Bull, squeezing behind the desk.

"COME IN," chirped Nippy Weston, hiding himself behind an upturned footlocker and switching off the light.

The door opened. A form entered.

Bam! The door slammed shut once more. A click told that it had locked. The newcomer stood motionless for an instant.

"*Whooooo!*" A moaning sound came from behind the desk.

"Wheeee! A higher pitched wail came from behind the upturned footlocker.

"What the devil—" That came from the lips of the one who had just entered.

From nowhere came the man-made ghost of glowing cheese cloth, dancing fantastically on the end of spring wire.

It came closer and closer to the stranger that the darkness hid. Nippy and Bull could just see his dim outline. But the darkness made it impossible for any recognition of person or rank.

"Whoooo!"

"Wheeeee!"

"Confound it, this is an outrage," bellowed a voice.

The *whoos* and *wheees* slowed and diminished. The ghost seemed to hesitate as he was about to clutch the newcomer. Something wasn't

THE BAT STAFFEL

right. There had been an air of authority in that voice.

"What's the meaning of this?" the voice demanded. "Turn on a light, someone."

The ghost disappeared altogether. A light flooded the room. Two very sheepish looking Battle Aces stepped from their hiding places and blinked at their commanding officer.

The colonel glared back at them, glanced about the room with a frown.

"What is this tom-foolery anyway?" he asked harshly. "You men going into your second childhood?"

Nippy stepped before him, squared his shoulders and saluted.

"My fault entirely, colonel," he said. "I just finished working out this trick. I was a magician before the War, sir. I didn't have any idea it was you, sir."

"No?" stormed the colonel, "Well, you'll have plenty of time to think it over. No passes for a week. I'd ground you two men if it wasn't for the fact that you're so confounded valuable in the air."

Bull Martin saluted.

"Yes, sir," he said.

Nippy Weston grinned slightly.

"If I might be permitted to raise the question," Nippy said, "was that what you came to see us about, sir?"

The colonel sputtered, reddened slightly.

"Er—not exactly. I came to learn whether you two men understand German or not."

Nippy Weston and Bull Martin stared at each other in a fog of uncertainty.

"German?" they both spouted together.

"That's what I said," stormed the colonel. "Do you or don't you? Don't stand there gawking like a couple of dummies."

Nippy got his head cleared first—as usual.

He nodded.

"Yes, sir. We both studied German together. Four years of it. We can understand it, but we don't do so well in speaking it. Bad accent, I mean, sir."

"But you do understand German?" the colonel pursued to make sure.

"Yes, sir," Bull answered. Nippy nodded.

The colonel turned on his heel and strode out the door, which opened before him by magic, as though the room was glad to be rid of the high command.

THE BAT STAFFEL

NIPPY TOOK a long breath. He raised the shades once more, turned off the light. Bull Martin sat down heavily on the cot of his smaller friend. The two stared at each other.

"Some day, wise guy," Bull growled, "you'll get us before a firing squad with those tricks of yours. My pal."

"Sorry," said Nippy and meant it. "But how did I know that was old eagle shoulders himself, instead of some orderly or greaseball? And wanting to know, do we understand German. Jumping Juniper, what's that got to do with the price of war babies?"

"Might make couple of dead ones out of live ones before we get through," Bull suggested dubiously. "Doesn't sound so hot to me, Nippy. I'll take my fighting on the wing and all that stuff and take my chances with the rest of the prop pushers. But when it comes to going over and making believe I'm a Heinie, unh-uh, not for me, kid. I'd die of the jitters before I got half started. And that's what it sounds like to me. Some kind of system to put us where we need to understand German."

Nippy nodded automatically.

"You know," he said, "I've been thinking. About that bird we got tangled with this morning. There's a queer one. Bull. He's dressed like a peasant. Got an old face as true as life and a broken nose like he's seen hard times or fists or something. But can he handle a sky rocket?"

He broke off in a laugh as he gazed at Bull Martin.

"Boy, if the gang back in the old college town could only see their pride and joy getting the royal razzberry of the air from a peasant with a broken nose and a face on him about fifty. I can imagine the headlines in the paper. Wouldn't the sports writers all over the States play that up. AGED PEASANT MAKES MONKEY OUT OF ALL AMERICAN HALF-BACK BULL MARTIN IN THE AIR.

"Say, listen, you little shrimp." Bull Martin bellowed. "I didn't notice you getting any palm wreaths for knocking the gentleman out of the sky. That was your idea in the first place, trying to force him down so we could satisfy our curiosity and make sure that everything was on the level. You got one up on me in Jerries on your score card, but I didn't notice that that helped you any with the boy friend with the crooked nose."

Bull studied the toe of his boot for a moment. He looked up with eyes narrowed.

"I've been trying to figure who that bird might be," he said. "Spy probably. And can he fly a sky crate!"

Nippy nodded. "And how." He studied Bull's square-jawed face for some time before he went on. "You know," he said at length, "I've got a pretty strong hunch. That guy we flew with this morning is no green rookie from Issoudon. He's a big shot in his line. His Spad didn't have any number or mark on it except the circles and red, white and blue stripes. But I'll bet a hundred franc note against a warped Hisso exhaust valve that this German-speaking business and that guy tied up together."

Bull nodded slowly.

"As usual, you're probably right. Nippy," Bull conceded. "Sometimes I think you're either psychic or just a fool for good guesses, you little shrimp."

THE BAT STAFFEL

"Psychic," corrected Nippy. "Look, I can even produce ghosts for the big cheese himself and—"

Knock-knock-knock! The sound shook the room.

"Come in," Nippy chirped, "and we're not fooling this time."

An orderly opened the door gingerly, peered in, then came through the door frame, saluted and handed an envelope apiece to Bull Martin and Nippy Weston.

"Special orders, sir," the orderly said.

Already the two were tearing the envelopes open.

The orderly left. Neither took his eyes from the orders before him.

They read:

> Special orders to First Lieutenants Weston and Martin:
> You are to take off at once in your Spads. You will bring with you clothing and personal belongings necessary for a stay of several days. Your main baggage will be moved later.
>
> Fly a straight course of one hundred and sixty-two degrees (162 degrees) by compass from your drome. You will pass the village of Ornas against the Jura Mountains. Continue straight on your course as above. Fly at two thousand feet until you can fly no farther. Then land.

The two Battle Aces stared at the signature. Reached it in their reading at one and the same time.

"Jumping Juniper," exploded Nippy.

"Holy Herring," bellowed Bull in awe.

And as though by a given signal they exclaimed together: "Special orders signed by the big shot himself, old J.J.P."

Together they got up. Nippy leaped for his foot locker. He yanked a few things out of it, stuffed them in a small leather bag. Some were magic properties for the amusement he loved; a few were such personal things as a razor, tooth brush and the like.

Bull Martin stood staring as though in a trance.

"Fly at two thousand feet until you can fly no farther," he breathed, half to himself. "What the—"

"Orders, you big ox," Nippy chirped. "And you notice it says we move at once, pronto. That means get going. I'm set now."

Suddenly Bull Martin turned and bolted for the door as though he had been abruptly blasted out of a trance.

"See you in five minutes," he called over his shoulder.

APPARENTLY, OTHER orders had come to the field. For without a word from either Nippy Weston or Bull Martin their Spads, 13 and 7, stood warm and ready when they met on the tarmac in front of their hangar a few minutes later.

Gun belts, oil tanks and gas tanks filled to capacity. Afternoon was lowering into evening. Together, the two studied a map of the region far to the southeast. There were plenty of miles between Colombey Les Belles and Onus. Nippy grinned as he folded his map.

"Well, big boy, here's hoping we find a place to squat when we can't fly any more on that course at two thousand."

Bull nodded seriously.

"And how," he said.

Hissos blasted. Spads 7 and 13 shot across the field, lifted

THE BAT STAFFEL

into the late afternoon sky and turned southeast, on a course of 162 degrees.

One, two hours they droned on along that course. Ahead they could see the Jura Mountains, and far to the northeast the Vosges towered.

Evening was falling fast. Great shadows filled the valleys and gullies as the sun sank lower and lower.

Nippy checked his altimeter constantly.

"Hum," he said. "At two thousand feet we'll swing right up that narrow canyon and run smack into the blind end of it."

For once the grin left his face. He looked over at Bull in his cockpit a hundred feet away. A puzzled expression was frozen on the square-jawed face of Bull.

It was growing darker as they settled deeper into the canyon. They held their altitude at two thousand feet, and the canyon walls rose about them.

Nippy held up two fingers to Bull in question. Instantly Bull glanced at his altimeter and held up two fingers in answer. The altimeters checked. Something would have to happen soon.

It grew darker and darker as the walls rose about them. The end of the canyon, the blind end, was growing narrower. They were forced to fly a little closer together. Once their wings almost touched.

It was so dark below that they could scarcely see the bottom clearly. They cast side-long glances at each other. The narrowness of the canyon demanded they keep their eyes constantly before them.

Once out of the corner of his eyes Nippy caught sight of

Bull. He had his fingers to his nose, holding it with an expression of disgust.

Bull's motor died as he cut the gun. Nippy reached for his throttle and pulled it back.

"I'd high-tail out of this mess if I could turn around," Bull shouted.

"Try and make it, "Nippy grinned. "Have to Immelman out and—"

His voice stopped. Bull had dropped lower and behind him. The blank wall at the end of the canyon had suddenly rushed at them out of the gloom. Both pilots stared, maneuvered their Spads, tried to figure some way out. There was no way except down, down in that dark pocket into which they could not see.

CHAPTER 7
THE SECRET DROME

NIPPY DROPPED the nose of his Spad. His grip tightened on the stick. Down into darkness. He turned for an instant in his seat and glanced behind. Bull was there, also nosing down. It was too late now to pull up and Immelman out of the narrow trap. Rocky projections hung out from the sides, making the passage dangerously narrow. There wasn't room to loop and roll.

Suddenly a light flared below two or three hundred feet distant. And in the flare they made out something astonishing. Something they had not guessed.

THE BAT STAFFEL

The canyon widened there at the bottom, where great overhanging rocks almost entirely hid the floor from the air.

A level field shone plainly in the light. The field was small but adequate. At one end stood another Spad. Near the flood lights, a pilot waited. He was waving them down.

Cautiously, the two kicked over and slipped in. The surprise, the sudden change, had left them gasping. Bull was first to touch wheels. Nippy was close beside him. Wheels rolled. The planes came to a stop. The pilot already on the field came trotting across to greet them.

Nippy Weston and Bull grinned as he faced them.

"You probably don't recognize me without the broken nose and the funny face," he smiled. "You're Nippy Weston and Bull Martin, of course, unless your C.O. lied to me. And you understand *Deutsches sprechen, nicht wahr?*"

Nippy nodded. *"Ziemlich gut,"* he admitted. "Fairly well."

"Good," said the third pilot. "And I suppose you'd like to know who I am."

"Like to," exploded Bull. "Say, listen. If you want a couple of birds on your hands gone crazy with curiosity, just keep up this secret stuff. You look like an old man one morning and turn into a youngster at night. Who the—"

"Pipe down and give him a chance," Nippy cut in. "And if you're getting blind, I'll tell you there's a set of captain's bars present."

G-8 laughed.

"Don't let that bother you," he advised. "I'm rather proud of my wings and bars, but I don't have to hide behind them for authority. You see, I earned these things before they advanced me to my present job. I had a name then. Now I'm sort of like a convict. I go by letter and number."

Bull nodded.

"I thought so this morning. A spy, eh? Well captain, you can take this from me. You haven't let your spying business interfere with your flying. I've heard a lot about a famous flyer who's a spy. Always wanted to meet him, but he's the biggest thing in the spy system, I understand. They call him G-8. I suppose you've met him, captain?"

The corners of the third pilot's mouth twitched.

"Yes," he said. "And so have you. You've both met him twice today."

"Huh?" gasped Bull. "You mean—"

THE BAT STAFFEL

"Sure," cut in Nippy. "I knew it all the time. You'd have known it too a lot sooner if you'd kept the ears open a lot more instead of the mouth."

Nippy turned and held out his hand to the master spy.

"G-8," he said, "this is about the proudest moment of my life, whether you believe it or not. But you've still got me curious. What is this, a game? This speaking German and then these orders for two thousand and all that stuff."

G-8 laughed.

"I'll say it's a game," he said. "The biggest game in the world. Listen—"

He told them then what he knew. About the story of the bats with their hideous poison breath.

"You see," he went on, "I've been studying up a little on caves. I found out about this place this noon and decided it would make a swell base for our work. But let's go over to the shack and get some chow. We can talk while we eat. We may go into action tonight."

TOGETHER THEY walked to a log hunting lodge, partly in ruins. A fire was crackling in a crude fireplace.

"Haven't much a variety of food," G-8 said as he fried bacon and eggs in a pan. "My man, Battle, will be up with the car tomorrow with all the supplies we should need for a time."

They ate, smoked, talked. G-8 went into more detail. He had Bull and Nippy sitting on the edges of their chairs listening.

"I found," he explained, "that there was a story about a great cave from which bats came and killed people with their breath along the Rhone valley. According to history—or legend—the great cave was covered by a landslide or a freak of nature. At any rate today it isn't just certain exactly where it was located. All the authorities agree, however, that it is within two or three miles of here—or rather that it was."

The square, hard jaw of Bull Martin protruded slightly.

"And you think," he demanded, "that this *Herr Doktor* Krueger has those bats trained to fly around blowing their breath in everybody's face?" He grunted in disgust. "That sounds like a lot of baloney to me."

G-8 smiled tolerantly.

"When you know me better, Bull," he said, "you'll know that I don't take much interest in fairy stories. I thought they were sort of silly things, even when I was a kid. But there's something

THE BAT STAFFEL

to this business of Krueger. I've seen about every kind of gas work that there is. But there's something different about this stuff Krueger calls the bat's breath. It's about the most potent stuff I've ever seen work. It does the whole disappearing trick in one act. Nothing left but dust."

Nippy leaned forward.

"I'd like to see it," he said. "I might put it in an act. That would be swell stuff for a magician until the cops came and he had to bring a pile of dust back to life."

Bull shivered. G-8 nodded.

"You'll have plenty of time to see it, I think."

He rose from his seat on a log beside the fireplace.

"I've picked you two to help me, in case you don't know why you're here," he said. "From now on we three constitute a spy system of our own. We have all the resources of the Allies at our command. When we get through with this job, there'll likely be another. You've seen me as I am. You've seen me in operation. You know as much as I do about this devilish bat menace."

He faced both Nippy and Bull. Glanced from one to the other. They were standing too. Tense, waiting.

"Unless you can think of a good reason for backing out," G-8 said, "we start now for the lookout five hundred feet above on the rim of the canyon."

He turned on his heel without another word and strode out into the pitch blackness of the canyon bottom.

Silently, Nippy Weston followed. And last, Big Bull Martin wedged his way out of the shanty door and strode behind.

G-8 AND HIS BATTLE ACES

DARKNESS WAS down over France and the great, bleak-faced Jura Mountains when they reached the top of the lookout G-8 had picked. No one had spoken since the climb had begun.

Cigarettes came out. G-8 struck a brequet and blew on it until it glowed dully.

"Keep the tips of the butts from glowing," he warned softly. "We might be within a hundred yards of the end of this tunnel, or we might be several miles from it."

From their perch high upon a projection of the canyon wall they could see across the leveler plane into France. Toward the east rose the Jura Mountains—mountains made even darker by the rising of a great silvery disc behind them that was the full moon.

For almost an hour they sat, moving only as they lighted fresh cigarettes and stomped out the old butts. Then Bull turned to G-8.

"From what you've heard about these bats," he inquired, "what's the slant on how they'll act, if it isn't all baloney?"

"I have developed a mental picture of the thing," G-8 said quietly. He pointed to the bleak face of the Jura Mountains.

Grimly G-8 tossed out a flare. It fell squarely on the back of the monster.

THE BAT STAFFEL

G-8 AND HIS BATTLE ACES

"Up there somewhere, according to the legendary story of the bats five hundred years ago, there's a mammoth cave. Of course *Herr Doktor* Krueger's yarn is crazy, as far as I'm concerned—that is, that the bats have lived for five hundred years and grown to immense proportions. However, its possible that he'll have planes—maybe Fokkers or Albatrosses or Pfalz planes—to fly over this area and spread the devilish gas. If that gets started there won't be any fun. I have some tanks of oxygen coming up with masks in case we need them. I'm hoping we can stop this thing before it gets started. Tonight we watch. Tomorrow, as soon as Battle gets here with everything, I go into action. You'll have your parts as well."

An angry, half-animal growl escaped Bull Martin's lips. He was pointing toward the level land where it stretched across the middle of France from the Jura Mountains. G-8 could see his big hands open and close convulsively.

"I'd like to get my hands on the throat of the devil that thought up this scheme," Bull rasped. "Innocent women and children out there!"

"I hope you get the chance," G-8 said. "I was in his castle this morning, but there wasn't time to do much with him. I thought I'd finished him when I threw him against the tank of gas. But he was shooting when I jumped out of the window."

Bull Martin said no more. Nippy Weston sat motionless for another hour, staring at the face of the mountain range two miles away. Midnight was approaching.

Suddenly Nippy tensed. His hand shot to the arm of G-8 who sat next to him. His other hand pointed.

THE BAT STAFFEL

"Look," he hissed. "Something! There. Seems to be flying."

CHAPTER 8
THE BAT PATROL

G-8 WAS on his feet instantly. All three were standing, staring toward the blank wall that was the side of the Jura Mountain range.

Something was moving in the moonlight. A great, strangely shaped thing that seemed to half float, half fly in the air.

And as they stared at the object, which was perhaps a mile away and could be seen but dimly in the light of the full moon, they heard a sound. A fluffing, flapping sound, slow and fluttery, like the murmur of giant wings.

The three stood frozen for seconds. Bull Martin was first to speak. His voice came in an angry bellow, as though to relieve his tension.

"Well, what we going to do, stand here and gawk at the thing when we've got ships to fly?"

G-8 had already started for the trail that led down into the canyon before Bull had finished speaking.

Scrambling, plunging, rolling, the three raced for their tiny drome.

They leaped before their Hissos. Spun the giant blades. Engines barked and roared into action. G-8 called to Bull and Nippy while the engines warmed.

"Listen," he warned, "this is tough, flying in the dark. Don't dare light a flare for they'll know where we're situated. Can both of you make it?"

For answer, Nippy Weston and Bull Martin sprang to their cockpits.

It was pitch dark in the bottom of that canyon, except for a shaft of moonlight that filtered in through the high wall. And in that light three Spads flipped their tails as they spun to head down the rock-bound passage. Hissos blasted until the walls echoed their roar with a deafening vibration of sound.

G-8 rose first. Up—up—up he climbed through that slit in the top of the canyon. Following the shaft of light Nippy and then Bull thundered their way after him.

Bull turned in his seat and stared from his rear position back into the chasm from which they had taken off. He shuddered uncontrollably at the thought of going back there in the dark. Then he turned to follow Nippy and G-8 out of the widening wall. They were above the canyon now. The three ranged the skyways with their eyes. G-8 pointed, blurped his motor to catch the attention of the other two. Dimly, they could see him gesturing higher above and to the south.

Nippy and Bull spun in their cockpits. Stared.

A giant object moved across the path of the moon. A monstrous thing that seemed to have a head the shape of a rat's and angular wings that either moved very rapidly or remained motionless, as though the great beast were soaring without effort.

Even above the roar of the three Hissos came a rhythmic

THE BAT STAFFEL

beat that filled the whole air. A sound that G-8 and Bull and Nippy could feel rather than hear.

Instantly, rudders and sticks moved. The three Spads banked and screamed for altitude. And as before, when the three-Spad flight had been returning from Germany that very morning, G-8 held the leader at point, and Bull and Nippy took their positions at left and right tips.

There could be no mistaking the beast of the air now. A giant bat was soaring there before them. The wings might be sixty feet in span. Great, wide wings they were, with legs coming from the middle section in the rear.

G-8 stared, then hurled closer, scrutinizing the monster through narrowed eyes.

Nippy Weston said: "Jumping Juniper, if I could produce an illusion like that I'd have the world by the tail."

Bull Martin shuddered at first, then let go an angry growl of rage and pressed his Vickers' triggers.

FLAME SPAT from his guns. G-8 warmed his Vickers as he tore in. Nippy Weston let go with a short burst.

The giant bat appeared to turn its head slightly and look at them. The ears were laid back. Great sockets seemed to be where the eyes should be.

But except for the slight movement of that grotesque head, the creature moved on with that hideous flapping sound.

The three pounced upon it at the same time from three different angles. Vickers rattled and bucked. White tracers slithered out like phantom ribbons in the moonlight. They ended in the wings and short, thick body of the giant bat.

Again and again those three Spads leaped and dove and fired and veered past, because their own speed was much faster than the speed of the bat.

But it was as though the monster of the air was feelingless, immortal. Never once did it change its course straight across France.

G-8 came down desperately for another attack on the body of the giant bat. Vickers steel sprayed across that form. He pulled back on the stick and sent his pellets up toward the head of the thing.

Nothing seemed to halt the monster. G-8 pinched himself to make sure he wasn't dreaming.

"I'm either crazy or else—" he snarled.

He stormed down again for another attack.

Bull Martin snarled across his nose in a wild dive. As he screamed past, he pointed toward the east.

G-8 turned in his seat, jerked upright. Two more giant bats were coming. Something like panic seized him for an instant. Fear was a feeling he never had known. But this trying to fight a thing you couldn't understand, couldn't kill or turn with machine-gun fire was something else. Something to drive a man insane, when the fate of the world lay in his hands and the world looked to him for protection.

Already Bull Martin and Nippy Weston had banked and were howling to meet those other two monsters of the air. Tongues of flame darted from their Vickers guns. But that was all that happened. Those, like the first, came on like automatons—as though nothing could stop them.

THE BAT STAFFEL

For a moment, G-8 was baffled. Then he sat up straight in his seat and groaned. For now he could make out a whitish blue vapor issuing from the nostrils of the leading bat.

Poison breath! The breath of the Bat! In desperation, G-8 roared over the back of the monster again and poured another burst of flaming Vickers lead into the body and wings. And again, nothing happened. The blue white gas continued to pour from the great holes in the nose at regular intervals.

Baffled, half-crazed in his helplessness, G-8 banked vertically and screamed back. His hand dropped beside him to bring out a flare.

His last resort. Perhaps that might do the trick. A flare might set fire to the thing, whatever it was, animal or bird or machine.

Back over the top of the beast he flew—his landing gear hardly ten feet above it. Grimly he tossed out the flare.

It fell squarely on the back of the monster—burst into brilliance. It burned with fierce heat, burned and smoldered and grew larger on the back of the giant bat.

G-8's heart leaped and sank again almost in the same beat. For, although the flare burned, it seemed to be doing no damage to the beast. The giant bat continued to fly along, taking no notice of the white-hot fire burning on its back. Presently the flare was caught by the wind and rolled off to fall down, toward the earth.

G-8 turned toward the other two. His stomach felt empty and jiggly; a great lump rose in his throat. Blue-white vapor was coming also from the nostrils of those other two bats.

Blue-white gas or breath that was heavier than air—that settled toward the ground rapidly.

Bull and Nippy had swung to one side as though they were ready to give up and just look on. G-8 could see their ships in the moonlight, hovering above the two rear monsters which were moving serenely across France, spraying their blue-white breath over the innocent folk below.

Then, just when it seemed that they would go on forever, unhindered, the first giant bat began to turn. A moment later the other two followed.

G-8 took a long breath. He tried to smile, but somehow a smile would not come now. Below him he knew that people were dying. A horrible thought. People dying and shrinking to merely a heap of ashes.

But something else became obvious. The bats were turning back. Now would be the chance to discover their hiding place. G-8 turned also. Bull and Nippy were following, zigzagging to keep pace.

MINUTES PASSED. The very air became tense. G-8 tried to be patient. Tried to whistle his pet tune, *Raggin' the Scale*. Somehow, his whistle wouldn't work. His eyes never left those bats beneath him. They were returning the way they had come, toward the blank face of the Jura Mountain range.

G-8 found himself leading the formation of three Spads. Bull and Nippy had fallen in behind him naturally. He was the recognized leader. It made him feel rather sick and weak to think of how little he really had to go on.

The bats were settling. They were going down into the shadow

THE BAT STAFFEL

of the mountain. They had been dim and uncertain enough in the moonlight. Now they were almost entirely merged in gloom.

In desperation, G-8 glided after them with idling motor until he was well in the shadow of the rocky cliffs. He could see very little. The bats seemed to be landing—but how—and where? He couldn't make out details.

Besides, he had scanned that mountain face this very afternoon. There was no hiding place in which they could find concealment.

Something moved before him. Moved down to where the bats had sunk into the black shadows. G-8 strained his eyes, glided closer. He'd have to open the gun again and use the motor before long. He was losing altitude rapidly—precious altitude.

He didn't want to alarm anyone who might be about. Otherwise he would have used a flare long before. But now he became, suddenly, insanely desperate. A flare came out of his cockpit and dropped over the side.

G-8 blinked and stared. He was too close to the ground for comfort. Another minute and he'd crash.

He slapped the gun open and the Hisso roared once more. He stared down as the flare burst into brilliance. Stared at the spot where he had thought those giant bats had landed. But only a level rocky stretch at the base of the mountain lay before him. Nothing more. No bats. No trace of them.

G-8 groaned and turned away. The flare had not yet burned out. He glanced about for Bull and Nippy, saw them some distance away headed back for the canyon.

G-8 AND HIS BATTLE ACES

G-8 frowned for an instant, then broke into a reluctant smile. Funny he hadn't thought of that too. He shot a glance at his gas gauge.

Empty!

That might mean what it said, or if it had just arrived at the empty point, it meant he had fifteen minutes more flying time. Bull and Nippy had apparently been watching their gauges more closely.

The moon had moved, so that its shaft of light now was shooting into the narrow canyon. Bull glided down first. Nippy next and G-8 followed.

But in spite of the pale light, it was tough landing down there. G-8 was coming in when he saw the wheel's of Bull's Spad touch.

The ship landed safely, rolled and stopped. Bull leaped out of his cockpit. Then he staggered.

Nippy was already down and rolling.

G-8 slipped, slammed down and coughed suddenly. His wheels touched. His lungs felt as though they had been blasted to bits. He knew his wheels were rolling now. He struggled for words.

"Block! Wheels!" he managed to yell.

Bull Martin had already tumbled over on his face.

"Open motors!" he shouted. "Don't breathe."

Nippy was already staggering, but he caught the idea. As rapidly as possible he placed stones under the wheels of the three planes, opened the motors to blow the gas out of the canyon.

THE BAT STAFFEL

Hissos throbbed. G-8, with bursting lungs, was making his way toward the cabin. A few minutes later he came out with one oxygen mask over his face and carrying two others.

He bent down beside Bull Martin. His fingers seemed thick—like thumbs. Nippy Weston was trying to help him—trying to put one of the masks on himself.

Then Nippy keeled over, too, with the mask only half on.

CHAPTER 9
THE VILLAGE OF DEATH

THINGS BECAME hazy before G-8's eyes as he blinked through the goggles of the oxygen mask. As swiftly as he could, he fixed one oxygen mask firmly on the square-jawed face of Bull Martin, then slowly, ponderously, he turned to Nippy Weston. His mask was partly off. G-8 managed to slip it back on, to fasten it in place, then he lay down on the ground to relax and allow the oxygen to do its work.

Things began to clear before his eyes. The three Spads were still running wide open, swaying against the rocks that had been placed under their wheels.

That meant that the thin fumes of the deadly hot breath which had settled in the canyon would soon be blown clear, and fresh air from above would be sucked in.

Anxiously, as G-8 lay still, he watched the other two forms. The big powerful body of Bull Martin and the smaller figure of Nippy Weston.

His eyes narrowed as he peered through his goggles. For an

instant he thought he noticed something queer about that big form of Bull Martin. It had moved. He was sure of that. But whether it had drawn together a little like the body of one in sleep, or whether a shrinking process had started, he could not determine.

Fearfully, he glanced at Nippy. The slim pilot had moved too. He had fallen doubled up. Now he was stretched out to a more comfortable position. Good sign. Nippy was alive.

G-8's eyes shifted to Bull again and his heart leaped. The big fellow was stretching out his legs now. That hadn't been a shrinking process after all.

Then, for the first time, G-8 realized that his muscles ached and his head throbbed. He made sure of the adjustments of the oxygen tanks and the masks on the three faces, including his own. Then he lay down close enough to touch either of the other two and closed his eyes while the shaft of moonlight vanished from the the floor of the canyon.

G-8 WAS awakened by someone shaking his shoulder and booming something that came faintly to his mask-covered ears.

He opened his eyes and stared up into the unmasked face of Bull. The big, square-jawed Yank was grinning.

"Hey, what is this?" Bull demanded. "A masquerade?"

G-8 sat up, took off his mask, unhooked the oxygen tank. Brilliant sunlight was streaming down through the slit of rock above. The bottom of the canyon at that moment was not an unpleasant place to be.

Nippy was sitting up, also rubbing his eyes and making faces as a result of just having wakened and taken off his mask.

THE BAT STAFFEL

"Masquerade?" he chirped. "Darned right it was a masquerade. Listen, you big ox, you came pretty close to being disguised as a heap of dust, as I remember."

Bull looked blankly from one to the other.

"Huh?" he exploded. "What are you two birds talking about?"

G-8 got to his feet and stretched luxuriously. Then he smiled.

"You were first down last night, Bull," he said. "You didn't realize that the bottom of the canyon had some of that bat breath in it until you got a small lungful. Then it was too late. I saw you tumble and that gave me the tip. I guess we managed to get the oxygen tank and mask on you just in time." Nippy was grinning. "Yep," he said. "Another minute and we'd picked you up in a dust pan.

"Course," he said, "a big ox like you would have made a pretty good heap at that."

Bull whirled and made a pass at his undersized friend. Nippy ducked under his arm, landing a resounding sock on the rock-like ribs as he flashed past.

"Hey, you two," G-8 laughed, "put some of that ambition into getting breakfast, will you? I've got some figuring to do."

He glanced at the three Spads standing with props stopped. "We're stuck here until Battle comes with my roadster and brings that truck load of supplies that's to follow. Ought to be along in a couple of hours or so. Meantime, I've got some studying to do."

While Nippy and Bull built a fire and began preparing breakfast, G-8 settled himself for his characteristic style of study.

He first wound tightly his portable phonograph on which he placed a repeating disc on his favorite record, *Raggin' the Scale*. Then he placed the needle in position and started the disc turning.

A bit squawkily, came the strains of the jazzy tune. Up and down the raggy scale the trombones and clarinets and saxophones romped.

The music seemed stimulating to the keen mind of G-8. His fingers began moving rapidly through pages of books that he had brought with him.

"Let's see," he mumbled. "Bat's Breath. The Curse of the Giant Bats in the Rhone Valley. Five hundred years ago the last attack of the bats is supposed to have taken place, according to peasant legend. There is nothing in authentic history to sub—"

Over and over and over ran that jazz tune as the repeater swung the needle arm and started the record again. Once G-8 leaped from his chair and wound the machine furiously. Then he dropped back to his seat and began drawing on a blank piece of paper.

Suddenly he looked up. Bull was leaning over his shoulder, watching.

"Well, what do you think about it?" G-8 demanded, grinning.

"Been thinking too much about it—I guess," Bull admitted, "since I came to this morning. I'd almost forgotten about those bats last night until I saw you working over your books."

The big fellow shivered.

G-8 laughed. "Just a lot of baloney," he ventured.

Bull nodded.

THE BAT STAFFEL

"Yeah. That's what I thought last night when you first told us the story. But I saw the brutes last night. And I haven't had a drink in two days either. There's nothing about those things that's baloney. They're real bats or—"

"You're crazy," finished G-8. "There's nothing in history to substantiate the story. Look here, though—"

He opened another book to a marked place.

"According to recorded fact the people of the Rhone valley were afflicted by a deadly plague in the year 1417. The legends of the peasants of the region carry the story that giant bats flew in droves from a great cave somewhere in the side of the Jura Mountains and their breath was deadly poison. Although this story is discredited as a myth, it is believed that the people of the Rhone valley did die in the year 1417 as a result of some natural phenomenon that caused a heavy-fog to settle over the valley. It is entirely likely that this fog might have contained an unusual gas, formed by the elements, that had a smothering effect upon human beings and caused many deaths."

Bull's face was growing purple and white by streaks.

"Baloney!" he rasped. "I thought I was a pretty wise bird last night. I laughed at the idea of giant bats. You said you didn't believe it either. But I saw them. You saw them. What do you figure out of that? What else can you figure than that they're real bats?"

G-8 shrugged.

Nippy cut in with a grin.

"Just the fact that they aren't real bats," he said. "Listen, you big ox, if I had the apparatus, I'd come close to duplicating those bats, and I'd do it with magic. Of course it would take some real man-sized apparatus but—"

"And make them fly through the air? Twice the size of our Spads," Bull retorted. "Don't talk like a lunatic!"

G-8 nodded.

"Nippy's right," he said. "I'm trying to figure out just how it could be done. I can't put my finger on an explanation of it just this minute, but I know there is one. I think we can be certain of one thing. They aren't real bats!"

Laying his book down, G-8 turned off the phonograph and got up. He thumped Bull on the chest with his fist and smiled.

"Come on, big boy," he cheered. "Don't let it get you. We're not fighting anything that isn't human-made. Bet on that and stop worrying about the supernatural—or whatever it is that's bothering you."

He turned briskly toward the door of the cabin.

"We've got a few hours before Battle and the truck will be here, if my guess is right," he said. "Let's take a walk out of this canyon. I'd like to get a look at Ornas, the town's about three or four miles from here—if you birds feel like walking that far. I want to see what effect this raid last night really had on the poor devils."

TOGETHER THE three Yanks swung out along the canyon floor and in less than an hour were entering the little village of Ornas.

A brooding stillness seemed to hang over the town. Nothing moved. No sound came from anywhere. No person walked

THE BAT STAFFEL

upon the narrow street. The village pump in the center of the square was deserted.

G-8 was a step ahead of the others. As they came to the doorway of the first house he stopped and stared in.

Bull and Nippy stared also. A gasp escaped the lips of the former football star—a gasp and then a low growl of anger.

For there, at one side of the open door, a little heap of dust lay. Flicks of the dust whipped up on the gentle breeze and drifted out into the stone-paved street.

"J-Jumping Juniper!" gasped Nippy.

G-8's teeth clenched. He shook his head.

"Poor devil," he muttered. "Some peasant sitting in the doorway, watching the moon. That's all that's left."

They passed on down the street. Before the village pump were two small heaps of dust. Perhaps most of the rest had been blown away by the wind. G-8 shuddered.

"Nice place," he said. "Let's go. I've had enough."

"You're telling me?" rasped Bull, already about facing.

"And I thought I was a magician," groaned Nippy. "Why, this guy Krueger makes me look like a piker."

They were moving out of the village the way they had come when Bull jumped suddenly, then very gingerly stepped around a pile of dust.

"What do you mean, magician?" he demanded a little farther on. "You still trying to make me believe that these bats are some trick put over by this nutty Krueger bird?"

G-8 whirled to face the big fellow at the edge of town. Bull was taller than he—taller and much heavier and stronger. But

G-8 AND HIS BATTLE ACES

G-8 placed his hands on the shoulders of the big Battle Ace and shook him.

"Listen, you," he snapped. "It isn't enough for the rest of us being on edge, I suppose, without you belly-aching about these giant bats being the real thing. That doesn't matter so much, anyway. The main thing is we've got to stop them. For my part, I wish I could be sure they were bats. Because if they're living things we could find a way of killing them. But if they're machines—and I'm making that guess—we've got a tougher job."

Bull purpled. He opened his mouth to speak, but there was something about the glare of those steel-gray eyes, the grip of G-8's hands, that held back his words.

"Maybe you weren't watching when I dropped the flare on the back of that first bat last night," G-8 went on. "An elephant is a pretty big animal. The body of that bat wasn't half the weight of a medium-sized elephant. An elephant would go crazy with a burning flare on his back. Magnesium is about the hottest burning stuff of its kind that there is. But did that bat show any discomfort? You were there. It never even winced. And that means one thing. It means that the back of that bat is made of metal. I'm sure of it. The flare would have set anything else on fire. Even the skin and fur of a real bat."

Bull nodded sheepishly.

"Sure," he admitted. "I—I guess you are right, G-8. Sure you are, when I stop and think of it. This bean of mine gets to working backwards sometimes. Sorry. No hard feelings?"

"None," said G-8 with a smile and a slap on the back.

But he stopped short after taking three more steps toward

THE BAT STAFFEL

the canyon. A low rumbling noise was coming from the other end of town.

ALL THREE turned and stared down the narrow main street—the street with little mounds of dust where the night before human beings had died.

A low, racy roadster swung into view, and behind it lumbered a big army truck loaded with drums of gas and cases of supplies.

Battle was at the wheel of the roadster. Two buck privates manned the truck.

A smile of pleasure and relief spread over Battle's face as he caught sight of G-8. The roadster drew to a halt beside the three.

"I'm that glad to see you sir," beamed Battle. "After passin' through about ten miles of villages and countryside, deserted just like this one, I was afraid fer you, sir. They say somethin' about bats and a gas attack last evenin', sir. I don't understand it, sir."

G-8 nodded.

"For once there's a lot of others who are as slow as you are to catch hold of an idea. In fact, we're mostly all with you. Ten miles, you say?"

"Yes, sir. We came through five or six villages in the last ten miles, sir, and all of them, sir, was deserted just like this one, sir. Deserted, with funny little heaps of dust about, like somebody had been cleanin' up the town a bit the night before and the heaps was waitin' for a wagon to come along and take the mess, sir."

G-8 gave a short nod, then turned to Bull and Nippy.

"This is Battle, my make-up man and aide. Hop on the running board. We're going into action at once."

He turned and shouted to the truck drivers.

"Get a move on that truck. Follow the roadster."

The roadster, under the hand now of G-8, whirled out of the village of Ornas and jolted over an old, unused road that led up the floor of the canyon. Some fifteen minutes later it rocked to a stop before the door of the cabin. Battle looked about, sniffing a little haughtily.

"Rather a nice place for a vacation, sir, if I may say so."

"Vacation?" snapped G-8. "Oh, yes, I did say vacation, didn't I? Well, forget that for now. We're going into our act again and right now, Battle. I'm about to become a *Kapitan* of the Imperial Air Force. Get out your stuff."

Battle grumbled at being hurried. But he knew his master. Hastily he selected a suitable German uniform from the baggage he had brought. Pots of makeup and plastic material were spread on a rude table inside the cabin.

G-8 was stripping off his clothes, by that time. He donned the German uniform swiftly and while he worked, he talked, giving orders to Bull and Nippy.

"I've got this figured out the best I can," he said. "We're not sure of anything much, except that things that look like bats fly about at night spreading death."

He glanced out of the door. The two truck drivers had finished unloading their truck. He called them in, scribbled hastily on a piece of paper, folded it and handed it to one of them.

"Thousands of lives depend on this order reaching headquar-

THE BAT STAFFEL

ters as soon as possible. It's an order for the evacuation of everything in France within a twenty-five mile radius of Ornas."

The private opened his eyes wide in astonishment.

"Gee, that's an order, sir!" he exploded.

"Right," said G-8. "See that that paper gets into the hands of the first American officer you meet. That's all. And don't spare that truck getting back."

THE PRIVATES left hurriedly. As the truck roared, Battle was beginning work on G-8's face.

"It'll take a close hair cut too," G-8 reminded his man, before beckoning to Bull and Nippy.

"Here are your orders," he said. "Remember where we saw those Bats disappear last night in the dark side of the mountain?"

The two nodded.

"O.K. Your job will begin tonight. Watch from the top of the canyon where we stood last night. See if you can figure out anything strange in the side of that mountain. Perhaps a great stone that rolls out on hinges—or rocky doors. Watch for anything.

"Tonight, you've got to take a big chance. You must get over to that level rock shelf where we saw the bats last. Stay there until something happens. Take an oxygen tank along, each of you."

He turned to Battle. "And that reminds me, Battle," he advised. "You keep an oxygen tank handy tonight. If you go to sleep, sleep with it on."

Then again to Nippy and Bull.

"See if you can discover how those bats disappear and where

they go. Of course if you find any way of exterminating them, don't wait for me. You'll have to work out your own fights. I'll be working on the other end of the line."

"The other end of the line," frowned Nippy. "I don't get you."

G-8 smiled through the make-up that Battle was putting on his face.

"Remember, Nippy, that pile of rocks on the north end of the island in the Rhine?"

A nod from Nippy.

"The more I've thought about that the more I'm convinced that there's a passage from those rocks to the tunnel through Switzerland. I think that's where our *Kapitan* went with his plans for the completion of the tunnel."

Both Bull and Nippy stared in astonishment at him. Bull shook his head.

"I wish I had your guts," he said fervently.

G-8 laughed. Battle was putting the finishing touches on his make-up now.

"I'll take the little case of make-up with me," he told his servant. "Might need it…."

To Bull he said. "You've got plenty of guts yourself, both you birds. That's why I picked you. And I think before we get through, we'll all need all we've got."

G-8 stood up and picked up a mirror.

"You two fill up Nippy's Spad. I've had a hunch that number 13 is lucky too, Nippy. You're going to play taxi driver for me. I don't want a plane around when I get on the island. Might be in the way, and I might—" he grinned—"come out of the tunnel

THE BAT STAFFEL

at the end where the bats come through. Get set. I'll be out in a minute."

CHAPTER 10
SEALED ORDERS

A FEW minutes later the Hisso of Spad 13 roared into action. G-8 stepped to the door of the cabin, ready, waiting. His hair was cropped close. He wore a German *offizier's* cap rakishly over one eye. A monocle was in the other eye. The make-up on his face was complete; it included two plain scars across the left cheek.

Even his air, his walk, was light and confident and jaunty, like that of a lordly Prussian *Kapitan* of the Imperial Air Force of the Kaiser.

Battle grinned and bowed as G-8 passed through the door.

"And if I may say so, sir," he called after him," you might give my regards to the Kaiser gentleman if you should see him, sir."

"Huh?" G-8 broke into a laugh. "Imagine that from you, Battle. Keep it up. You're coming. And—" he flung the last over his shoulder as he walked toward the waiting Spad—"don't forget what I told you about that oxygen mask, Battle, or you won't ever know anything, specially from then on."

"Thank you, sir," came the answer. "And good luck to you, sir."

Bull and Nippy grinned at the sight of G-8 togged out as a German *offizier*. Heels clicked. They snapped up smart salutes. G-8 answered in his best warlord manner.

93

"*Haben sie fertig Gemacht?*" he demanded. "Have you finished? Are you ready?"

"*Jawohl, Herr Kapitan,*" they answered together.

G-8 nodded at Nippy.

"Not so bad," he complimented. "Would you mind lying out on the wing yourself and letting me fly your ship? You see I don't want to take a chance of getting this uniform spotted with oil. They might suspect if they saw a spotted outfit on a *Kapitan*, These Heinies are nuts for neatness."

"O.K. with me," Nippy agreed. "I'm ready to ride the rods any time you say the word."

G-8 climbed into the cockpit. Nippy clambered to the right wing and stretched out on the step, holding fast to wires and struts and letting his legs trail off the rear edge.

The Hisso blasted. The Spad shot across the field and climbed out of the narrow-topped canyon.

Twenty minutes of roaring to the north; then the Spad circled. G-8 stared down from his cockpit. Two thousand feet below, the Rhine River gleamed and shimmered in the sunlight. He was directly above the island where he and Nippy had landed the morning before.

Instantly, he reached up and cut the switch. No need of any more noise than necessary. He glanced down at Nippy on the wing below him and the little fellow grinned back.

"You don't waste any noise when you land," he suggested in a half whisper as they glided down.

"Not when I'm landing in Germany, Nippy," said G-8.

He was sitting up straight in his seat, staring ahead, weaving

THE BAT STAFFEL

this way and that in the seat to make sure that he was seeing everything around the field. The field looked good. He made out the scorched end where the Albatros had flamed the morning previous. Suddenly, a little to the left of that spot, something else caught his eye.

He blinked and stared hard at it. Something was showing through those trees. Something that was green like the trees but that had a rough cross in black marked against it.

"Nippy," he hissed. "Look over there. Tell me what you see."

Nippy glanced up, followed pointing G-8's finger.

"An E.A. looks like to me. Enemy aircraft. What's the idea?"

"That's what I'd like to know. Got to move cautiously."

Nippy grinned.

"And we got to land too. Don't forget that. We got about three hundred feet left. Let's see you get the Hisso started in that altitude."

"We are going to land," G-8 said. "But have your automatic ready. This doesn't look so hot."

The Spad glided down. The wind was blowing up the river from the north. That made it unnecessary for G-8 to fly over the enemy plane they had spotted in hiding.

Wheels touched and the Spad rolled to a stop.

INSTANTLY, LUGER in hand, G-8 was out of the cockpit. Nippy slipped from the wing, clutching his automatic. Half crouched, they ran across the field toward the half-hidden enemy plane.

G-8 was first to break through the brush and reach it. A Fokker D-7 was concealed there. No one seemed to be about.

G-8 AND HIS BATTLE ACES

"See," hissed G-8. "That bears out my hunch. This island is one of the entrances to the great tunnel. They contact by airplane with headquarters."

He jerked his head toward Nippy's ship, started to run back.

"Hop in and I'll give you a whirl on the prop. Got to get you and that Spad out of here before the owner of that Boche crate shows up," G-8 ordered.

Nippy leaped into the seat. The prop spun. Hisso roared. The tail whisked and the Spad spun. It roared down the field, turned into the wind and took the air.

G-8 ran back the length of the field. He broke through the trees and stopped at a high point from which he could command a good view of the great tumbled rocks that composed this end of the island.

There he crouched and waited.

Minutes dragged by like years. G-8 remained calm, cool, self-possessed. Perhaps these were the qualities that made him such a great spy. Always the mere donning of the uniform of the enemy country brought self-composure. That utter self-confidence that comes to few.

The minutes dragged into an hour. The sun settled lower in the west. Afternoon would soon be turning to evening. Complete stillness was over the island.

Several times G-8 flattened an ear to the great rock that was his lookout. He did so now, listening intently. Suddenly every muscle of his body grew rigid, he had caught the dull tread of feet.

He lifted his head. He could hear another sound now. A

THE BAT STAFFEL

scraping, treading sound. Someone was coming. Someone was walking confidently along a stone paving. He could hear the clink of hard heels. There seemed to be some labor to the tread. As though the walker were climbing up from a lower level.

G-8 flattened himself on the rock. His eyes roved over the tumbled expanse. Nothing moved. Only that one sound came to him. That sound of a buoyant tread.

Suddenly, he froze where he crouched. Something had moved before him. A German *offizier* had stepped out boldly into the bright sunlight.

He had come from an opening directly below the great boulder on which G-8 lay!

The *offizier*, a *Kapitan*, blinked for a moment; evidently the change of light had blinded him. He hesitated—passed a gloved hand before his eyes.

G-8 tensed for the spring. He must move swiftly. Must take every advantage possible. Still, he would fight fair.

"Ach, das ist besser," the German muttered to himself, blinking again.

At that moment, G-8 leaped. His Luger was in its holster and he did not draw. He came down with bare hands. The German crumpled beneath his savage dive. G-8 leaped to his feet again, and as he did so he jerked the Boche upward.

The *Kapitan* stared at this strange assailant who also wore the uniform of a *Kapitan*.

"*Gott im Himmel,*" he exploded. "You *dummkopf.* You have gone crazy?"

A right closed his mouth. A hard left buried itself into his stomach. Uph! The *Kapitan* doubled over with pain.

Again that right of G-8 came up and smacked him on the chin.

The eyes of the German glazed. He tottered. His powerful hands clutched G-8 for support. Then, still clutching him, he wavered, stood up again. He was a giant in strength, although about the same size as the Yank.

His head seemed to be clearing now. G-8 fought to break that iron hold on his arms. But he seemed powerless to do so for the moment. The German *Kapitan* glared at him, holding him at arm's length.

"*Donnervetter!* What does this mean? I go on an important mission. Another *Kapitan* of the Imperial Air Force leaps upon me and fights like a—"

G-8 put every ounce of his strength into the wrenching jerk. The German's hold slipped and the Yank was away like a flash. He tensed. The Boche was reaching for his Luger. That must not be. No gun fire on that island. It might be heard by other Germans in the tunnel below.

No gun fire!

G-8 sprang for the Luger which was already half drawn. His left clutched the Boche's hand; his right came up from knee level, swishing as it zipped through the air.

Smack! There was dynamite behind that blow to the chin of the German *Kapitan*. Again the eyes glazed. The hand that had held the Luger went limp. The knees began to fold up.

G-8 drew back his right fist and put his whole force behind

another blow. This second uppercut lifted the heavier German as he was about to drop limply. It lifted him to his full height and then hurled him in a heap against the side of a great boulder.

There was a dull, hollow sound as his round head struck solid rock. The body went limp altogether and piled in a heap.

INSTANTLY, G-8 was making a hurried examination of the pockets. He found a long envelope; jerking it out he examined the writing on the outside.

> His *Excellenz,* General von Kuhl
> From General Ludenheim, commander of underground forces in the east.
> By Special messenger, *Kapitan* Schlosser.

G-8 was still breathing hard. He turned and gazed at the crumpled heap that had been *Kapitan* Schlosser.

Then he slipped the envelope into the inside pocket of his own coat. Bending over the still form, he felt for movement where the heart should be. There was no movement. Blood was oozing from a gash on the head.

G-8 glanced at the crevasse between the stones from which the *Kapitan* had emerged and shook his head.

"I'm afraid, Schlosser, you're entirely too close to this in case someone else should come along," he said, half aloud.

He picked up the limp form and carried it around a large rock to another chink between two boulders. There he placed the body back on the stones.

Then carefully he made his way farther north. He must be alone, safe from possible discovery for a time. Finding a suitable niche, he sat down calmly, produced a tiny kit of bottles and ink and pen and spread them out before him.

A simple touch of the liquid from one bottle and one end of the stolen envelope became unsealed. The wax seal was untouched.

Eagerly, G-8 opened the end flap and drew out the papers. There were some drawings. Drawings of a tunnel. The instant his eye took in the lines, an indelible print was made on his alert brain.

The northern mouth of the passage was located in a wood just north of the Swiss Border. The other end he had already guessed—was five miles from the French village of Ornas near his own canyon airdrome.

On the map it was marked *CAVE OF THE BATS*.

Glancing over the map once more, he calculated the tunnel was fully twenty miles long. It seemed unthinkable. Studying the layout further he noted other things.

"Old Mine," was printed at one point. *"Cave of the Bats,"* was long and large in size, running a great distance under the ridge of the Jura mountains.

After several moments, he opened the typewritten sheet.

General von Kuhl:
Excellenz:
We are ready for the great surprise attack across France. At present we have fifty thousand of our picked troops, together with sufficient guns. They are lodged in the tunnel, awaiting the breath of the bats to sweep the way clear for them. This

THE BAT STAFFEL

trick of the bats seems to be working admirably. Already that *verdammt* spy, G-8, has lodged himself with several assistants somewhere near our outlet in the side of the mountain. He saw our gas work last night. We had hoped that we would kill him and his assistants, but apparently such was not the case. Our Intelligence in France tells us that he has sent orders for the evacuation of France for twenty-five miles about Ornas. We are already working to learn his hiding place. We also expect to have a trap ready tonight when he comes to investigate the place where the bats land.

Orders, then, from the High Command are to advance a hundred thousand troops to the mouth of the tunnel. Our fifty thousand men will be moving over France, beginning tonight, as soon as the Bat's breath has been spread and has had time to clear away with the wind.

You, *Excellenz*, will hold your hundred thousand men ready until 1 o'clock P.M. tomorrow, at which time you will march them through the tunnel and out at the other end through the opening from the Cave of the Bats and across France to Paris.

Thousands of our men will follow. The war will be won for the *Vaterland* in twenty-four hours.

Hoch, Excellenz.

Signed   General Ludenheim.

G-8 SMILED slowly when he had finished. He rubbed his chin meditatively.

"I'll say you're optimistic, anyway, Luddy, old boy," he said. "Let's see. A hundred thousand and fifty thousand. That would make a hundred and fifty thousand. Sure. A hundred and fifty thousand men stuck in a long necked bottle—if it works."

He glanced at the words, 1 o'clock P. M. in the second from the last paragraph. From his store of tiny bottles, he brought a dropper. Dipping it in the liquid, he placed it on the letter P.

Instantly, the letter vanished. Still smiling, G-8 blew until the paper was dry. Then with pen and ink he replaced the typed letter P with an A which made the orders read—

> "You, *Excellenz,* will hold your hundred thousand men ready until 1 o'clock A.M. tomorrow, at which time you will march them through the tunnel—"

He held the typewritten sheet off at arm's length and surveyed it with satisfaction.

"Better," he said softly to himself. "That twelve hours ought to make all the difference between life and death to a lot of people."

He slipped the papers into the envelope once more. With the liquid from another tiny bottle he resealed the end flap, and surveyed the effect carefully. There was no trace of the envelope having been opened.

He got up and walked lightly to where he had left the *Kapitan.* The body was just where he had placed it.

Turning the face toward him, he studied it carefully. Then from an inside coat pocket he brought a miniature makeup case, set it before him, and began working on his own face.

Swiftly, some of the make-up that Battle had put on came off. His nose flattened slightly at the tip. One scar on the right

THE BAT STAFFEL

cheek and two on the left appeared to match those three scars that were plainly visible on the face of *Kapitan* Schlosser.

Finished, G-8 rose and surveyed himself in a small pocket glass. He smiled.

"*Herr Kapitan* Schlosser himself," he said softly.

He bent down beside the still form once more and went through the pockets completely. He found identification tags, passes for *Kapitan* Schlosser—and a single word written on a card:

"hund"

The German word for dog. Perhaps a password. He studied it for a moment, nodded and finished his examination of the pockets.

G-8 hesitated now. He seemed to have all the information he needed, yet there was something else he must know. Where would he find this General von Kuhl?

Slowly he walked toward the waiting Fokker. But as he reached it an idea seized him. Plunging his hands into the pocket at the side of the cockpit, he found papers, which he brought out.

They were maps of the eastern Front and of Germany north of Switzerland. Examining the first one hurriedly his attention was attracted by the mark "X" north of Freiburg—the town named for the old castle on the banks of the Rhine.

Freiburg. Sure. He remembered seeing an airdrome there some time ago. A small, unimportant airdrome it had seemed when he had seen it from ten thousand feet.

He'd try it.

He slipped the map back in the side of the cockpit and heaved the tail of the Fokker about. Two, three pulls at the prop and the Mercedes started with a roar.

He taxied slowly down the field to warm the engine and turned into the wind. Ready! He pushed open the gun. The engine thundered before him. The Fokker leaped along the ground, grew light and lifted.

CHAPTER 11
G-8, SPECIAL MESSENGER

G-8 FOLLOWED the general course of the Rhine River as it twisted through the mountainous country. Ahead he saw Freiburg castle on its rocky point. He smiled, as it crept beneath him and he could look straight down on the tower—and the great jagged roof and the court where he would have been shot.

"What a fit that little buck-toothed devil, *Doktor* Krueger, would have if he knew I was flying this Fokker right over his head," G-8 chuckled. "And what a headache I'd give him if I had a load of bombs."

He turned then toward the town of Freiburg. It was a small place with comfortable houses scattered here and there on rambling roads or streets. But the town itself was not what held his interest.

On the south side, where a level plain ran to meet the sharp

THE BAT STAFFEL

rise of the mountains, acres and acres of ground were covered with tents.

G-8 slowed the speed of his ship and took in the scene in detail. Thousands of men were down there. The men waiting to be sent into the tunnel. The men mentioned in the letter that he now carried!

He pushed the gun open and roared on over the great camp. A half-confident smile crossed his face. If everything worked properly, those men would be on the move for the mouth of the tunnel before long.

He looked again carefully, but couldn't see a sign that would indicate the north opening of the main tunnel. Perhaps it was somewhere in that wood beyond.

Nodding, G-8 turned forward in his seat. Later he would find that north entrance. Something much more important was before him now. He must deliver his message. He wasn't even sure that he was heading for the headquarters of General von Kuhl. Well, he'd have to find out.

He shrugged as he roared over the town. The Fokker's nose dropped and the engine ceased it's throbbing drone as he sighted a small airdrome just north of Freiburg. As usual his memory had been correct. Boldly, he dropped to a lower level and prepared to land.

Only one hangar was on the field. A few German mechanics appeared and watched him land, G-8 taxied importantly to the tarmac and cut his motor. An *Unterleutnant* approached and saluted.

G-8 was ready with his test opening. Was he in the right

place? Had he guessed correctly? Did Schlosser land here to deliver his special messages?

"*Ach,* they have even more soldiers in the camp than they had when I left, *nicht wahr?*" G-8 said in his perfect German.

A tense moment while the *Unterleutnant* scrutinized him. A brief, split second of time that seemed like an eternity to G-8, while he waited for the answer that would tell him whether he was in German or Dutch. The *Unterleutnant* seemed puzzled for that instant; then he smiled and bowed.

"*Jawohl!* They come more every day, *Kapitan* Schlosser."

Somehow the heart of G-8 seemed to make better work of it from then on. His breathing came easier too. But the *Unterleutnant* seemed still puzzled—hesitant.

G-8 noted it instantly. He cracked a broad smile in contrast to his first gruff, but not unpleasant, manner.

"*Ja. Das ist gut.* Soon they will go into the tunnel, *ja?*"

He winked slyly at the *Unterleutnant.*

Instantly the doubt on the young *Unterleutnant's* face fled.

"*Jawohl, Herr Kapitan.* That makes me feel much better. Always before when you land with special messages for his *Excellenz* you are laughing. You say we will soon win the war. So today when you land just now you seem to have changed. I was worried. Perhaps something had come up that I did not know. Perhaps this G-8 devil that we hear about had—"

G-8 had his cue. He chuckled deep down in his throat and thumped the *Unterleutnant* on the chest.

"*Ach.* Did you not hear? We have laid a trap for *Der Verdam-*

THE BAT STAFFEL

mte G-8. Perhaps already he is captured. I assure you you need not worry."

G-8 glanced quickly about the hangar.

"But the car! I must hurry with this special message from—"

He stopped short and followed the finger of the *Unterleutnant*. It indicated a large staff car half-hidden by the corner of the hangar.

"As always, *Kapitan*, it waits at the corner of the hangar. Have you forgotten?"

Again for the instant there was a slight suspicious tone in the voice of the young *offizier*.

G-8 turned and took a few steps toward the car. He turned back suddenly. He could feel the eyes of the *Unterleutnant* burning his back with uncertain gaze.

"My verdammte Mercedes," G-8 flung at him. "It has worked badly coming over. You know I am not myself when I have engine trouble. It is constantly on my mind. Have it fixed at once. Check the magnetos—and the timing to make sure."

He turned abruptly again and strode toward the waiting staff car.

THE DRIVER saluted beside the open tonneau door. G-8 cracked a slight smile as he answered and stepped into the car. The door slammed. There had been no hesitancy on the part of the driver in recognizing him. G-8 felt better.

As the car rolled out of the airdrome and gathered speed toward Freiburg, G-8 ran over what he had learned about *Kapitan* Schlosser. He had assumed from the general appearance of the fellow during their short association that he was the gruff, snooty, Prussian type of *offizier*. On the contrary, he was apparently more of a jovial type. So that would be it.

On entering the car, G-8 had smiled only slightly in answering the driver's salute. That seemed to have gotten by. He had not even given orders as to their destination. The driver hadn't asked. G-8 wasn't volunteering any information that wasn't required.

The town of Freiburg as they swung down the main street was filled with *offiziers* and men. Hundreds of them. There seemed to be a significant tenseness in them as the car swung to a stop before the largest building. It was as though someone had said, "In that car comes the Special Messenger with orders for our movements. Where do we go now?"

G-8 felt the prickle of a thousand and more staring eyes upon him. Not one of his movements was missed.

The driver leaped from his seat and stood at attention with the tonneau door open.

G-8 stepped from the car and strode up the steps without an instant's hesitation. A single pause as though any of this was new to him and he was lost.

A guard at the door of the building presented arms and partly barred G-8's entrance.

G-8 saluted and took another step as though he was used to walking into the place without being stopped, except for the slight formality of salute.

"You may announce *Kapitan* Schlosser to his *Excellenz*," he said.

"*Jawohl!*"

THE BAT STAFFEL

That worked. The guard wheeled and strode inside the main door. G-8 followed close behind.

Not once did the guard turn and glance back. He paused at the third door on the right down the main corridor of the building and knocked.

A booming voice said: *"Kommen!"*

The guard opened the door, stepped inside for an instant. There were voices. Then the guard stepped out again and stood at one side to let G-8 pass.

G-8 was inside. The door closed behind him. Instantly he was at his utmost calm. General von Kuhl, gray-haired, and mustached—the latter waxed at the ends in an upward thrust—gave him a nod.

Heels clicked. G-8 snapped his salute.

"Ach, Kapitan Schlosser! You bring the most important papers. Give them to me at once. The time I believe is nearly here."

G-8 flipped the papers from his pocket and handed the sealed envelope to the general. A tense minute or two passed. The Yank watched every expression, every movement of the facial muscles of the general.

There might have been a flaw in his change of letters in the message. He could not be sure. Nothing was sure in the war while working with code—or straight messages for that matter. One of the opposite side could never tell when code was being used that looked like a regular message.

He breathed a little more deeply when von Kuhl glanced at the map, smiled slightly. A moment later he looked up.

"The end of the war will soon come, *Kapitan*," he nodded.

G-8 AND HIS BATTLE ACES

THE BAT STAFFEL

G-8 AND HIS BATTLE ACES

"A victory for the *Vaterland* is well in sight. Perhaps not many hours away. Return to his *Excellenz, Herr* General Ludenheim, and tell him he shall have his extra hundred thousand men in the tunnel at one o'clock tomorrow morning. They are outside now awaiting my command to move. Hurry your return. His *Excellenz* will be expecting you. *Das ist alles.*"

Heels clicked once more. G-8 snapped his salute, about-faced and strode from the room.

OUTSIDE IN the corridor he heard footsteps behind him. Someone following—too close for comfort. It was hard not to break into a run, to keep his even pace while those steps, coming with apparent stealth, crept closer—closer.

Smack!

A hand slapped him on the back, sending him forward. He leaped to catch himself and whirled, fists clenched, ready for anything.

A roar of laughter echoed through the corridor. A big, powerful German, also in the uniform of a *Kapitan,* was doubling over with mirth at the sudden savagery of G-8.

"Ach, you are funny, Karl Schlosser! How you turned around so quick and mad. I saw you come from von Kuhl's office just now and—"

The *Kapitan* paused for a moment and the smile faded from his face. He stared hard at the Yank.

G-8 broke a smile.

"Ach, you gave me a start," he confessed. "But I must hurry. Again in a day or so I will come and then have more time."

Without answering, the big *Kapitan* stepped around in front

THE BAT STAFFEL

of G-8, and for another brief moment he studied him. There was uncertainty written on his face—uncertainty and suspicion.

"You are getting jumpy, Karl," he said gravely, "and your voice sounds strange. I trust you are well?" That was a trace of sarcasm.

G-8 stopped. No use trying to push his way past this persistent friend of the genuine *Kapitan* Schlosser. The master American spy nodded and shrugged nonchalantly.

"As well as staying in that *verdammte* tunnel will permit," he answered. "I have a bad cold and I must hurry now. This tunnel is getting me jumpy. I must hurry now, old friend. I only wish I could stay and have a drink with you."

G-8 took another step to go around the larger man. But the face of the powerful *Kapitan* grew darker. He placed strong hands on G-8's shoulders and before the Yank could duck, spun him about.

G-8 jerked loose instantly. Fighting his way out must be the last resort. He must bluff—or else—

Something of a plan flashed through his mind as the *Kapitan* opened his mouth to speak. This was obviously a very close friend of Schlosser's. Rottenest luck possible. "You are not *Kapitan* Karl Schlosser," the other was saying in a voice that could be heard the length of the corridor. "Who are you?"

CHAPTER 12
A CORPSE DISAPPEARS

THE SOUND of clattering boots sounded from the rear of the hall. Two *offiziers* were striding up to see what the argument might be.

Cold that seemed far below the zero point zipped down G-8's spine. Clammy sweat poured out under his arms and ran down his ribs. But outwardly he was calm.

"*Was ist los?*" demanded one of the *offiziers*, barging into the argument.

The other stood ominously near, a Luger in plain view.

G-8 was thinking with lightning speed.

"Shhhh," he said holding his finger to his lips. "Must this be ruined because someone is a pig-head? I can explain, but we must find an office where we will not be overheard."

The big *Kapitan* turned and jerked his head toward a half-open door. G-8 felt the prod of a Luger in his back. He entered. The others followed. The last *offizier* closed the door.

"Who are you?" the big *Kapitan* demanded. "You are not Karl Schlosser. I know that. You have made up well. Perfectly except for one thing. There is no scar behind your right ear as there is with Karl. I remembered seeing the lack of it when I came up behind you. I know that scar well. I put it there myself five years ago when Karl and I were dueling in our last year at Heidelberg."

"Who are you?"

G-8 glanced about the ring of three *offiziers*. Three Lugers

THE BAT STAFFEL

were aimed at him. Against the odds, he forced a smile. He winked then at the big *Kapitan*, who didn't seem to appreciate the joke.

"Listen," he hissed. "I do not think anyone has suspected but you three. No, I am not Karl Schlosser. But I know him well. I met him first in special air assignment around the Belgian Front. Then I was transferred to special duty with the Bats."

A glance from face to face showed he wasn't getting very far. He struggled on, laughing as he spoke. G-8 was the perfect example of self-confidence.

"Last night Karl got very drunk on some special old wine that was found in the old mine. You know the kind. Smooth as velvet but suddenly bursts like a bomb shell. Karl did not know until too late that it was—high explosive. *Vesstehen sie?*"

G-8's eyes flitted from one face to the other. The Germans saw only laughter in those eyes—not the tense desperation behind. The laughter got a reaction. The big *Kapitan*, who seemed the closest friend of Schlosser, grinned.

"And you know how wine with a kick like that stays sometimes for two, three perhaps four days," G-8 hurried on hopefully.

"Ja, ja," nodded the *Kapitan*. The other two *offiziers* were smiling now.

"Karl could not come with the special message," G-8 continued. "I have had much experience in make-up. I am about his size. I am perhaps the best friend Karl has in the tunnel. So it was my idea that I come in his place. He is asleep and very dizzy."

That was the end. Grinning, he watched the three faces for

the reaction. It came in a burst of smothered laughter. The big *Kapitan* slapped him on the back for the second time. Again he laughed after the slap. But this time G-8 felt much freer.

"You are a friend of Karl Schlosser, you are a friend of ours, *Herr Kapitan*," the other beamed. "Especially of me, *Kapitan* Krantz."

G-8 grinned and nodded.

"*Danke*," he said," and now I must hurry back. A slip-up on my part and Karl will be suspected. So far, with the exception of you *Kapitan*, I have passed everywhere as Karl Schlosser. Now I must return to General Ludenheim with the message von Kuhl has sent him."

The others turned toward the door with him. They were laughing as he departed.

"*Auf wiedersehen*," G-8 waved.

"*Auf wiedersehen*," came the answer, with three chuckles attached.

The guard at the door presented arms as he passed. Not until he was being driven out of town, away from those preying eyes, did he take a full-sized breath—only to check it again when the car turned in at the airdrome.

For the *Unterleutnant* was striding toward him—with a guard at either side—guards with rifles and fixed bayonets!

THE CHAUFFEUR leaped from the car and opened the door. Deliberately, G-8 stepped out. He kept his hand close to his holstered Luger as the *Unterleutnant* came to a stop before him. There was a moment of tense suspense—then the *Unterleutnant's* voice:

THE BAT STAFFEL

"*Kapitan* Krantz just called on the phone, *Herr Kapitan*."

A pause during which a million thoughts seemed to crowd G-8's already busy brain. Krantz, the *offizier* who had discovered his masquerade because of a small scar that wasn't behind the right ear. Had they changed their minds and suspected—

"*Kapitan* Krantz requested a guard for you, *Herr Kapitan* Schlosser," the young *Unterleutnant* went on. "I do not understand. But the *Herr Kapitan* Krantz said it was to be a guard of honor to your Fokker."

It was hard for G-8 to contain himself. The sudden relief was almost overwhelming. These German *offiziers* with their jokes and their deviltry as well! Much like all other soldiers.

G-8 managed to laugh—just a deep-throated chuckle. He hardly dared allow himself more than that for the moment.

"Krantz is a great joker," he said.

He strode toward his warming Fokker with a guard on either side. It gave him a queer sensation. Something like having a friend hold a loaded and cocked revolver at one's head in fun.

The two guards presented arms as he climbed into the cockpit. Mechanics pulled the blocks from in front of the wheels.

G-8 slapped the gun open with the heel of his hand and kicked the rudder. The Mercedes howled. The Fokker spun and droned into the wind—and air.

He climbed south. Minutes passed and then the island was again below.

He thrilled at the thought of entering the tunnel at last. Of actually going through it from end to end. Perhaps—if he lived that long—he would see the cave of the bats! Would find out what the bats were! What this trick was, spoken of in the secret orders.

He cut the gun and brought the Fokker down to a gentle landing. Rolling it to its former hiding place, he got out and lifted the tail about until it rested where it had before. Then he made his way toward the heap of rocks.

Before entering the passage from which *Kapitan* Schlosser had come, he picked his way to the spot where he had left the German's body.

Suddenly, he stopped stock still, staring before him. Blood marked the side of the rock where the Boche's head had lain. But only blood was there. The body of *Kapitan* Schlosser was gone.

CHAPTER 13
THE TUNNEL

G-8 GREW tense as he stood there before the place where *Kapitan* Schlosser had lain. He glanced at his wrist watch. He had been gone a little more than an hour.

Bending down, he drew a finger along in the blood. It was fresh, just beginning to thicken. The body couldn't have been moved more than fifteen minutes or possibly twenty.

Body!

The idea suddenly smote G-8 a stunning blow. He had concealed Schlosser where he was reasonably sure no one would find him. He had felt of the heart. There had been no beating as far as he could tell.

THE BAT STAFFEL

He leaped to his feet.

Body!

Perhaps *Kapitan* Schlosser hadn't been dead. He couldn't swear to it. Of course his heart had ceased to beat to all appearances, but there was no assurance of certain death.

He stood rigid. A sense of danger crept over him. A sense that he could not explain or describe.

His first warning came with the gentle scraping of a boot heel on stone. He spun around. His hand flashed for his Luger. His eyes focused on a bloody figure swaying a little against a great boulder.

Kapitan Schlosser himself stood there a Luger in his hand! Anger and hatred flamed in his eyes.

G-8 paused in his reach for his gun. He froze for but a split second. Training, natural ability and perfect self-control came to his aid instantly. He dropped his hands to his side and broke off in a laugh that sounded genuine.

"Ach, Kapitan Schlosser, you startled me. You have been hurt. Hurt, do you understand? An airplane."

Schlosser shook his head as though to send the fog from his brain. But the Luger remained trained on G-8.

He stared hard at the master spy. His eyes, clotted with blood from the wound on his head, narrowed to slits.

"What is this, another trick?" he bellowed. *"Ach! Mein kopf!"*

G-8 nodded. His face took on a serious look.

"Yes, that is the trouble, *Herr Kapitan,*" he said. "Your head. Perhaps your memory has been affected."

"Memory," Schlosser rasped. "Memory. *Ach, Himmel.* Could

I forget that fight with you? The blow you strike with your fist? And now you come back and find my body gone. I recognized you from behind. *Gott,* I am looking at myself. Your face. It looks like mine. *Ach, was ist los?*"

"Your head," insisted G-8. "That's what's the matter. Don't you remember? I saved you. I saved you from death when a diving *verdammte* airplane plunged at you with machine guns spitting lead. You were struck a glancing blow on the head by one of the bullets. Then, while you lay unconscious, I took your papers to General von Kuhl at Freiburg."

FOR THE first time *Kapitan* Schlosser seemed to waver. His free hand crossed his eyes and forehead as though to sweep away cobwebs that had formed there.

But his gun hand still clutched the Luger and held it trained on the middle of G-8's stomach.

"You—took the special orders to General von Kuhl?"

"Jawohl," smiled G-8." Of course. I found them upon you. I knew your name by the name of the envelope. I knew they must be of utmost importance, so while you lay against a rock I took the papers to von Kuhl. I have just returned. I was overjoyed to find you had gotten up from where I had left you. Believe me, *Herr Kapitan,* it was a pleasure to know that one so brave as you had not been killed as I feared when I left you at first."

Schlosser continued to look puzzled.

"You say, *Mein Herr,* that you saved me from attack by an enemy plane?"

"Jawohl. See? The side of your head is hurt and bleeding. One of the Vickers bullets nicked you in the *kopf* and knocked you

unconscious. I pulled your body back beneath some rocks where they could not see you from the air."

Schlosser seemed to dream for a moment. The Luger wavered. G-8 pointed upward. He moved a step closer to Schlosser.

"See? The plane—it was a Spad—was coming in a power dive from up there just as you came out of the entrance to the tunnel. You heard them and looked up, but the sunlight blinded you. They opened fire. I chanced to be here and jerked you back behind some rocks."

Schlosser nodded heavily.

"*Ja*. That is a good story, perhaps. But—"

He seemed half willing to believe. As he finished he glanced into the sky for an instant's meditation and thought. As though to picture the diving airplane.

G-8 moved instantly. A short step. A kick with his left leg that came up so fast it could hardly be seen.

Crack! His boot struck the heavy wrist that held the Luger. At the same time G-8's hand leaped to his own Luger. *Bam-bam-bam!* The Luger leaped and spat flame.

The eyes of the *Kapitan* opened wide. His mouth opened too, as though he were going to speak. But only a grunt came. His head dropped on his chest and he pitched over on his face.

G-8 leaped forward. He reached the falling Luger before chance clutching fingers might reach it. But there was no movement about the body of *Herr Kapitan* Schlosser now, except that twitching that comes before death.

Blood oozed out. The muscles ceased their twitching. The form relaxed, limp and lifeless.

G-8 AND HIS BATTLE ACES

G-8 found a hole between the rocks and slid the body into that improvised grave. He examined his hands. They were covered with blood. That must not be.

He climbed over the tumbled mass of rocks to the river's edge and washed thoroughly; then he returned, took another look at Schlosser's body—which was partly hidden from view except from straight above—and made his way toward the tunnel entrance.

Before entering he reviewed his name—his lines. *Hund* was the password somewhere. He'd give it if he was challenged. He smiled.

"So General Ludenheim is expecting me, eh?" he murmured. "Well, he'll get an earful before long, if I have luck."

Without further hesitation, he stepped down into the black crevice from which he had seen the *Herr Kapitan* Schlosser climb less than two hours before.

ALMOST AT once he came to an abrupt turn in the rocky opening. Then, the passage seemed to widen slightly as though it were man-made from that point. He felt his way along in the dark. The walls were damp and clammy. The passage was going down, down. Of course it must if it passed under the river.

His hands touched a dead-end wall and he fumbled at the side. Muffled voices came from his right. He turned. Against the gleaming wetness of the wall he could see the dim shimmer of light reflected from another passage.

He searched it, turned left and came upon a lighted corridor.

THE BAT STAFFEL

Far down this level passage were soldiers. German soldiers with Lugers at their belts.

G-8 never slackened his pace. To hesitate was to be lost. He strode toward them, his boots resounding on the stone floor. He must be under the river. The walls about him now were of concrete.

Two guards stepped up, their hands resting on their Luger butts. There was a sign of recognition on their faces, but in spite of that fact, the one, a sergeant, demanded:

"Halt and give the password, *Herr Kapitan*."

"*Jawohl,*" smiled G-8," and how *ist deiner Hund* today?"

The sergeant grinned, snapped a salute and stepped aside for him to pass. G-8 answered with a salute and strode on down the corridor.

He heard the sergeant chuckle and say something about a jolly *Kapitan* who could joke about the password. G-8 smiled to himself. If that sergeant knew how tense he had been within when he had tried the password!

He had walked for perhaps two hundred yards when he heard a rumble of voices from ahead, punctuated by the squawking of a phonograph that was playing some sort of dreamy waltz.

The noise must be in the main tunnel. He was astonished that it was so close to the Rhine and the island.

When he reached it, no guard was there to stop him. He stood for a moment and blinked in the stronger light of a large cavern-like room. The ceiling was low, but the passage was wide. Here and there were posts holding up the ceiling, like the shores that hold up the roof of a coal mine.

At once the thought dawned upon him. That section of the map that had been marked "old mine." This must be part of it. A clever study of geology had made this tunnel possible by a minimum of work.

By short connecting passages this deserted mine had been joined to a giant cave farther to the south—all put together to form a tunnel beneath the Swiss Alps into eastern France.

In front of him German soldiers rested or wrote or read. There was an air of confidence—of certain safety about the place. Three young soldiers were singing the words to the tune that rasped from the phonograph.

G-8 strode out among them. They leaped to their feet at once. They were enlisted men and non-commissioned officers—and he was dressed as a *Kapitan.*

He smiled and waved them back to their positions, wondering just where he would find the office of General Ludenheim. But that didn't really matter. Not yet. Perhaps Ludenheim might have another special mission for him to go upon. But he wanted to see more of this tunnel now.

The tunnel widened and narrowed as he strode on. Everywhere soldiers leaped to their feet as he approached. Everywhere they waited orders to move—to go into action.

There was a light-hearted buoyancy about the place. Now and then he would hear a soldier say in passing—

"In twenty-four hours the *Vaterland* will win. The war will be over!"

And the thought of his own plan made him shudder a little. These Germans. Not a bad sort. Young men. Youngsters. Kids.

THE BAT STAFFEL

But they must be stopped. They and the fiend behind them that was threatening the world with destruction.

This was war. Already that vapor, called the breath of the bat, had killed thousands of innocent peasants—old people and children—in just one raid!

IT SEEMED as though he had been walking two, three miles. The passage changed in appearance. It no longer resembled an old mine. Like that section beneath the river, the walls, ceilings and floors were of concrete, and the tunnel was narrower—although large enough to permit the passage of trucks and guns. It was perhaps ten feet high and a little wider.

A blast of forced air blew constantly through it for ventilation. It seemed to come from ahead. That would be from the south end.

He knew that his muscles were getting sore and stiff from walking so far in the damp, underground passage. He must have walked miles already.

Suddenly, he came upon the end of the concrete passage. It widened into a mammoth stone enclosure—high ceilings, wide expanse, irregular floor.

During his long walk, he had seen only a few German soldiers. Now he suddenly found himself looking at many of them. As in the old mine, they were lying about, talking, resting. Waiting.

A separate room had been blocked off to his left. The sides of the cavern were of rock, but this separate place had been built of concrete. It stood aloof like a private set of offices. Guards paced before the door.

G-8 paused in the shadow of an overhanging rock for a

moment and studied the passage, before him. That would likely be the offices of General Ludenheim. Worth a try anyway.

He straightened. Brought himself up to his haughtiest Prussian pose. The general would be expecting a reply from von Kuhl. There would be investigations if he did not receive it before long.

G-8 knew the danger of failure. A false move and he was finished. There was no backing out now that he was within the great tunnel. He knew of but one entrance or exit. There were others, of course. Two at least. But they were as good as useless to him if he were found out. No passage would do him any good if suspected. Telephone systems that must run the length of the tunnel would head him off from any direction.

The prickly nervous feeling along his spine only lasted during the space of time that he was striding from the mouth of the concrete tunnel to the guards on duty before the apparent office.

Two guards stepped before him. They too seemed to recognize G-8—or think that they recognized him.

"*Kapitan* Schlosser to see his *Excellenz,*" G-8 said.

CHAPTER 14
CAVE OF THE BATS

ONE GUARD nodded.

"I will see if his *Excellenz, Herr* General Ludenheim, will see *Kapitan* Schlosser," he announced.

He turned on his heel and strode off into the office. A moment later he came back and saluted.

THE BAT STAFFEL

"His *Excellenz* will see you at once, *Herr Kapitan.*"

G-8 saluted. He strode confidently past the guards into the office. The prickly sensation had fled. He was himself again. Coldly calm. Confident.

His heels clicked as he snapped to attention before a scar-faced, clean-shaven general with close-cropped head. Ludenheim was younger than von Kuhl. An *offizier* of the newer militaristic school.

His face hardly moved as he said—

"You have delivered the papers?"

"Jawohl, Excellenz."

"And what did von Kuhl say?"

"He requested me, *Excellenz,* to tell you he will be ready—with his troops at the time specified. He also sends his compliments."

A short nod from Ludenheim. Not the slightest change of expression on his poker face that G-8 watched so closely for the first sign of suspicion.

"Gut. Heraus mit. I will send for you when I need you once again. *Das ist alles."*

Heels clicked again. That snapped salute of G-8 looked like the real thing. He pivoted in perfect German style and strode from the room.

Outside he saluted the guards as they presented arms at his passing. He walked on with business-like stride through the great, vaulted cavern. It seemed to run on and on into endless rocky walls and domes of electrically-lighted space.

All about, men waited. Tension in the air. Guns, large field guns in rows and rifles stacked everywhere waiting for the signal.

G-8 AND HIS BATTLE ACES

G-8 glanced at his watch. It would be dark in another hour or so. Not long to wait. He strode on.

The cavern turned abruptly as great underground caves formed by nature are apt to do. Instantly the cave grew larger. Startlingly so. He paused for an instant and gaped at the spectacle.

Great bat-like things hung, head downward from the high, vaulted ceiling. He slowed his stride, stepped to a wall and stared for a moment without interruption.

Three of these bat-like things hung from above. Men on scaffolds were working on them. There were cables and steel arms and machinery everywhere. A big German *offizier*, a *Kapitan*, was shouting orders and directing the preparations.

G-8 thrilled at thought of his success so far. But he had only begun with his work. For some minutes, he watched the big *Kapitan* directing work on the monsters. He couldn't tell much about them except that now he was positive that they were not real bats. That he had suspected all along, to be sure; but he had never, until now, been certain.

Strange, mysterious-looking machines they were. Even at close range with lights playing upon them it was hard to tell them from genuine giant bats except for the fact that men worked about them, oiling joints and making adjustments.

That *Kapitan* in charge. G-8 wanted to talk to him. But the way must be paved properly. He stopped a Leutnant in passing.

"That *Kapitan, Herr Leutnant*," he said. "I can not recall his name. The one in charge of—"

He stopped short. The *leutnant* was staring at him with a puzzled frown. Those searching eyes.

THE BAT STAFFEL

"You do not know *Kapitan* Fritz Muzzen, *Herr Kapitan* Schlosser?" he demanded in astonishment. The eyes narrowed. Instantly G-8 replied.

"*Ach*, Fritz. My eyes. *Danke.* I thought that was he but I could not be sure. *Jawohl.* Of course. My eyes and the dim light in here."

G-8 blinked and rubbed his eyes strenuously.

"The changes of light for me from daylight to this. It is hard for me to see—lately."

The *leutnant* saluted, and passed on. G-8 caught a glimpse of him some distance away. He was staring back. A prickle of uncertainty crept up G-8's back.

A GONG sounded behind him. The officer who had been designated as *Kapitan* Muzzen turned at the sound and came directly toward him. Catching sight of him, he swerved in his course. A grin spread over his big round face.

"*Ach*, Karl. At last you have come to accept my invitation," he beamed. "But first let us eat together. *Kommen!*"

"*Ja*, I have come Fritz," G-8 chuckled, "but I am not sure about accepting your invitation. I am very busy you know."

Fritz grabbed G-8 by the arm and led him in the direction that was now being taken by many officers, most of whom were beneath their rank. Fritz Muzzen laughed.

"But it is not all business I fear that keeps you away," he chided. "You should be more cold-blooded. After all this is war. We shall eat, and then I shall explain the workings of the bat machines—and then tonight you will fly one of them. Think what a thrill it will be to travel in the moonlight and know that

G-8 AND HIS BATTLE ACES

when you turn on the gas valve you are killing thousands of *verdammte* French!"

They reached a quarter of the cave where the ceiling was lower. Where tables were set in long rows and men were sitting down amid the chatter of voices and the clatter of tin ware. They found seats. Sat down and helped themselves to food— black bread and beans and tough canned meat.

G-8 sighed.

"*Ja*, Fritz. I have been thinking the matter over. Perhaps you are right. I—"

A messenger stepped behind Muzzen and whispered something in his ear. Muzzen sat up straight for a moment, rose, bowed to G-8 and excused himself.

Slowly, without causing notice, G-8 turned his head and watched out of the tail of his eye. His whole spine seemed to freeze at what he saw.

The *Leutnant* of whom he had asked Muzzen's name was standing, waiting for the *Kapitan* who was striding toward him. Instantly, G-8 turned to his plate again. His brain spun. He tried to make a good show at eating. He heard footsteps behind him. If he was trapped, he was trapped. Only one pair of feet were booming behind. He glanced up into the serious face of Fritz Muzzen.

Instantly, he blinked. Blinked several times and rubbed his eyes hard. Muzzen, his eyes upon him, was sitting down once more.

"I was saying when you left," G-8 went on casually where he had left off, "that I have suffered myself lately. Perhaps that

THE BAT STAFFEL

is one reason why I am losing my happy disposition and getting serious about this war. My eyes are, as you might say, going back on me. A dose of hot oil from a broken line two days ago."

That split second when Fritz Muzzen continued to study him seemed ever-lasting. G-8 managed somehow to laugh.

"Why do you look at me that way, Fritz?" he demanded. "Is it a crime to have eye trouble?"

Then, like the bursting of a flare, Muzzen's face broke into a grin and he laughed.

"*Dummkopf,*" he snorted. "The *leutnant* just told me that you asked him my name. As though you would have to if you could see perfectly with no eye trouble. *Ach,* that *leutnant* is a crazy, suspicious fellow."

"This war makes one that way, especially the very young like him," G-8 ventured as they continued to eat.

He pushed back his plate finally and half rose.

"I haven't much more time, Fritz before Ludenheim may be wanting me. And I came down tonight to have you explain the working of the bat machines and the gas. Perhaps I will be able to get permission to fly in one tonight. We shall see when the time comes nearer, *ja?*"

Fritz Muzzen nodded and rose also.

"*Ja,* let us go." They walked toward the bat cave together. "It is always a pleasure to explain these clever inventions."

THEY TURNED into the great cavern of the bats. Muzzen pointed at the three hanging bat machines. At rows of gas tanks under high pressure standing against the right wall.

"There," he said proudly. "And all the invention and plan of

Herr Doktor Krueger. *Ach,* he is a clever one. And best of all is that gas called the 'Bat's Breath.' *Das ist a gut one.* Of course it is no more the breath of a bat than those machines are real bats. It is a clever gas that *Herr Doktor* Krueger has discovered. You have heard how it works?"

G-8 stifled a shudder.

"Jawohl," he said. "That gas must be hard to handle in here, since we have no gas masks to guard against it."

Muzzen shrugged.

"Kill or get killed, *das ist war, ja!"* he said. "But it will soon be over, this war, then perhaps with the aid of *Herr Doktor* Krueger and his gas and more bat machines we can conquer the world. With this—" he pointed about the great cavern—"he can control the world—or exterminate the people into piles of dust."

Kapitan Muzzen laughed in a rasping voice.

"Deutschland uber alles, nicht wahr?" he shouted. "At all costs. What do the lives of other peoples mean if the *Vaterland* wins?"

G-8 forced a grin and nodded in agreement. He turned and stared from the tanks to the bat machines hanging high above.

"There," smiled Muzzen, "are, as, you know, the three bats that will spread death before us as we march across France. Their whole structure, bodies and wings are of a new metal, very light and very strong. They are fireproof. They fly very slowly, but are in no danger of attack."

G-8 blinked as he stared upward. The light was very dim inside the cavern except where men worked with electric cables running to lights close by. G-8 was glad. Perhaps he might not

THE BAT STAFFEL

have gotten away with the masquerade before this friend of the real Schlosser had the lights in the mess and the cave of the bats been brighter.

"But I do not see any power plants. No engines," G-8 probed.

Muzzen laughed.

"Even you are fooled. That is more of the story of the giant bats and their deadly breath. All mechanical. All man-made. The invention of the great *Herr Doktor* Krueger. In this light you can not see them and in the dark of night it is even more difficult. The two engines in each, super-Mercedes, are located where the feet should be. Pusher engines at the backs of where the wings fold. You will notice that the eyes are very close together. Those are the shielded cockpits. Two pilots may be carried, although we used but one pilot each last night in order to carry more of the heavy gas. It is impossible to shoot a pilot except straight through the big eye of the machine. Is that not clever, Karl?"

G-8's jaw bulged for an instant. He nodded.

"Very clever," he said. "But are we sure that the Allies can do nothing to cause our plans to fail?"

Kapitan Muzzen was laughing in his rasping cackle.

"You have heard of G-8, the great American spy?" he asked.

G-8 tensed. For the moment he could hardly hold himself from leaping away and reaching for his Luger. But instead he turned slowly and eyed Muzzen.

"Heard of G-8?" he said in a little astonishment. "But who has not heard of that *verdammt* one, Fritz."

Muzzen laughed again.

"But he will be famous little more," he chuckled. "Already he has played into our hands. He believed the story of the bats that *Herr Doktor* Krueger told him yesterday. He escaped then, clever devil, and with two others, he is hiding somewhere in this sector with planes. He attacked our bats last night—he and two assistants. But he failed in his attack. One of our pilots recognized his Spad in the light of a flare that was thrown by this *verdammt* G-8 on the back of one bat machine."

G-8 looked surprised. He smiled.

"So? Das ist gut. The devil should be killed."

"*Jawohl*," grinned Muzzen. "But listen. He will be killed tonight. G-8 and his two aces are about to be trapped. They will come here tonight to try to learn more about the bats. They will be outside on the level rock plain. They will wait to see where the side of the mountain opens to let out the bats. We have a trap set for them. We only await darkness and their coming."

CHAPTER 15
TRAPPED!

WHEN NIPPY WESTON took off from the island where he had left G-8, he turned south. But he didn't go straight back to Bull and Battle in their hide-out on the canyon floor. Instead he swung over the village of Ornas and dived low.

The usual smile that was a habit with Nippy was gone as he looked down on the barrenness of the small town. His eyes

THE BAT STAFFEL

caught sight of the tiny piles of dust, most of them whipped flat now by the breeze. His teeth clenched and he whistled his plane back toward the mountains.

Diving low here, he skirted the level rock floor in front of the great mountain. His eyes searched for signs of openings, but he could find none. He shook his head, baffled.

"Swellest trick I ever saw and I've seen a couple," he mumbled. "Wish I had a disappearing act like that. Bats the size of barns, just sink into the side of that mountain without an effort. Boy, what an illusion. If I could pull one like—"

Abruptly, Nippy sat up in his seat. He was roaring back along the face of the mountain, staring down at the rocky tableland some hundred feet below him. His Spad number 13 was cocked over on one ear, making a turn for the canyon, when his eyes caught peculiar marks in the rock surface. The marks were in a semicircle curving outward from the mountain. Like the scratches made by a door, the bottom of which rubs the floor.

Instantly, Nippy kicked and pulled. The Spad groaned and banked on the other ear, coming around for another dive at those strange markings.

"Hum," Nippy mused as he looked down on the marks for the second time. "Ain't that somethin'? Not such a hot illusion from this angle. But maybe they didn't plan the show for an audience up in the top balcony."

This time he saw two sets of scratches. Two sets that came in together close to the face of the mountain.

As he hurled past he took one last look backward, then he turned for the canyon.

"Unless I'm crazy," he breathed, "those scratches are from a great door opening. The one we're looking for—but it's about the cleverest piece of camouflage I've ever seen."

He slammed down through the narrow-slitted canyon opening, cut his motor and prepared to land. He saw Bull walking out on the little floor of the canyon as he came down. Saw Battle running anxiously to meet him as he landed and rolled.

"I trust you left the master quite well, sir?" Battle inquired in deep concern.

"As well," Nippy grinned climbing out of his cockpit, "as a Yank can be dressed in a German officer's uniform and at large behind the German lines."

Bull Martin shuddered.

"No job like that for mine," he said emphatically. "I'll fight what comes and take my chances. But that stuff of not knowing when you were going to be caught and snuffed out in front of a stone wall hasn't any appeal."

They were walking toward the cabin. Battle was hurrying ahead. The smell of food came to them from the open door. Good, well-cooked food.

"Funny," Bull said again, "but we've only been with this guy G-8 a few hours and still, now that's he's gone, there's a hole in this outfit as big as all outdoors."

They sat down and began to eat. Nippy nodded.

"Does leave a vacancy," he admitted. "Swell guy, G-8. But we got our orders and—"

"And I could pick out a lot of jobs I'd rather do," Bull ventured.

THE BAT STAFFEL

"This chasing bats, not knowing what they are or anything about them except that you stay dead when they blow in your face, doesn't help the nervous system any."

Nippy grinned.

"Maybe you thought you were coming on a vacation when you came up here," he cracked.

Battle cut in from the side lines.

"Come to think of it and beggin' your pardons, seems I did hear the master say something about this being a vacation in the mountains."

"And speaking of vacations," Bull said, "how about digging me a couple more spuds, Battle?"

"Very well, sir."

The plate returned filled. Bull finished and pushed back his plate. He handed Nippy his cigarettes, took one himself and struck a match.

"What's the next move?" he asked when that was finished.

"A nice long walk is good after a meal," Nippy grinned. "In words that you can understand, we're going mountain climbing."

He told Bull then of the scratches he had seen from the air. The big Yank's eyes widened. He rose from the table.

"Let's go," he said. "Sounds like something to look into."

THEY CLIMBED up the same trail they had taken at night when they had gotten their first sight of the bats. Once on top of the canyon wall, they picked their way toward the flat rocky tableland and the mountain it skirted.

A low, wooded valley separated them from the rocky plain that ran from the face of the mountain. They struck off through the wood, dropped into the valley and a half hour later came up cautiously on the other side where the valley ended at the rim of the tableland.

For some time they lay in the brush at the valley's edge, watching the face of the mountain. Nothing moved. No sound came. Only that bleak face staring at them.

"There," Nippy pointed to the place below which he had seen the scratches. "That's where the cave opens unless I'm crazy."

Bull drew his automatic.

"I'd like to prove that you are, shrimp," he grinned. "Come on. We'll take a look."

Boldly, each with an automatic held ready, they strode out across the open tableland. The scratches were just as Nippy had seen them from the air; they swung in two arcs from the cliff, circling out from the middle of a great slab of rock.

Bull looked blankly. He shook his head, and listened. He studied it, caught hold of what might be a separation and pulled with all his might. No sound except his puffing and snort of disgust.

Nippy clutched his arm, drew him away. They walked to the middle of the long, tableland, which was smooth and even, like a great natural pavement.

"We could land here with a cinch," Nippy said, "after dark."

Bull snorted in disgust.

"And get about as far as we did last night—if you're thinking of chasing bats."

"Yeah?" snapped Nippy leading Bull on back the way they had come. "Well listen you big ox, I got a hunch and it'll work.

It just came to me. Did you get a good look at the eyes of those bats?"

Bull looked blankly. He shook his head.

"Why, no."

"You wouldn't," Nippy chirped. "I couldn't make out anything but the hole where the eyes should be. If these bats were real we'd probably get along best and surest by trying to shoot them directly in the eyes. But since we can't see anything but holes let's work on the hunch just the same. We've peppered them with Vicker's slugs about every other place."

Bull grew enthusiastic.

"Say, that's an idea," he boomed as they dropped into the wooded valley. "We'll land here tonight, hide our planes in those trees at the south end of the plateau and sneak back. We can lie low and see how everything works. See how the bats get out and then when we've got that information, we'll get to our crates, catch up with the slow-flying birds—or whatever they are—and give 'em what it takes, eh?"

"Yeah?" Nippy grinned. "All your idea, eh? Swell pal."

THE CANYON floor was dark but still the after-glow of the waning day showed through the slit far overhead. Another hour. Then gassed and amunitioned Spads number 13 and 7 droned into the air and rose out of the slit above the canyon.

Together they climbed into the darkness. Climbed toward the west, away from their objecture. If anyone were watching or listening they would not guess that the Spads were turning back later.

Guns were cut at almost the same instant, then switches. The engines died and the noses dropped as the ships turned in circles and headed back with no other sound than the wind breathing through the wings and rigging.

Wheels touched minutes later. Touched and rolled far down toward the end of the rocky pavement. Bull and Nippy leaped from their cockpits, and one by one, wheeled their Spads under the trees a little way ahead.

They turned and started back.

"Best to lay low for a while and watch what happens," Nippy suggested.

Bull grunted.

"Right. Have plenty of time to reach the ships and get 'em started before the bats—or whatever they are—get too far, the rate they fly. Going to be a clear night. Have a moon again around midnight."

"And one thing I want to see is how they work this stunt of opening up a mountain and spitting out those big things," Nippy said. "Maybe I can get an idea for a new trick."

"You and your tricks," Bull scoffed. "You'll never grow—"

He stopped short and crouched suddenly. Nippy was down beside him in the darkness. Bull was pointing. Not with his finger but with the muzzle of his automatic.

"Something moved. Just ahead," he hissed.

"Saw it," Nippy answered.

Bull turned slowly and looked behind, toward the ships.

Blam! Blam! Everything happened at once. Bull's gun exploded. Nippy's did the same. Figures were low to the ground but moving in behind them, between them and their ships. A wild scream of pain came from one throat and a grunt from another out there in the darkness. Then abruptly the whole night about them was flooded with light from beams in a circle at about fifty feet.

Completely surrounded!

Bull whirled like a caged animal. A bellow of rage escaped his mouth. His automatic spat and spat again. Guns crackled from every side. The lights blinded them, but still Bull kept his bearings for their ships.

Head down, half doubled, he charged in that direction.

"Let's go!" That was Nippy's tip to follow like a shadow.

Nippy was fast as lightning. Bull had surprising speed for one of his size and weight. He charged that south line of lights and blazing guns in the old zigzag course that had made him all-American half, had carried many a ball over the line in spite of odds.

In his left hand he squeezed the automatic until the magazine was empty. Germans fell before him. Bullets screamed past. He plunged through the weird light like a dynamic-legged cannonball with a flashing terrier at its heels.

Germans grunted and fell back before that brutal straight arm. On and on he ran. Germans came running from the side. Sprang up before their rush. Many Germans. There seemed to be no end to them.

On and on plunged that former football star with Nippy following like a weaving tail. Lugers spat just before them. Flame darted at the spot where they had just been. Then:

Blam!

Something smashed Bull on the head with the force of a sledge hammer. He stumbled, plunged on in a half instinctive roll, and slumped limp.

Nippy stumbled behind. He tried to dodge and keep from falling. Germans seemed to be all about them, smothering them. He felt himself going down with what seemed two tons of humanity on top of him. Then things faded as his head struck the hard surface of the rock and inky blackness came down over him.

NIPPY OPENED his eyes to a gentle swaying motion. He was being carried. He stared about, half sat up in astonishment and peered upward.

"Jumpin' Juniper!" he exploded. "The bats."

He stared about for Bull. Heard the sound of machinery and saw the giant stone doors closing behind them. They were inside the cave! Then he saw Bull. He was just coming to. Blood oozed from a gash on the side of his head. A skin wound it seemed to be. Bull saw him at the same time.

A *leutnant* beside Nippy grinned at him. They were setting both prisoners on their feet. Letting them walk under guard.

"Jawohl," the *leutnant* said. "The bats, *Mein Herren*. You have seen them in flight, *nicht wahr?*"

He turned abruptly to Bull, glanced again at Nippy.

"Which one of you prize prisoners is G-8, the American spy?" he demanded.

Nippy looked at Bull. Bull looked at Nippy.

"G-8?" piped Nippy. "One of us, G-8? That's a hot—"

He stopped short. Bull cut in with—

THE BAT STAFFEL

"Never heard of him. A spy, you say?"

"*Ach, Dummkopf!*" exclaimed the leutnant. "Come. We shall see. We go now to his *Excellenz,* the general."

Nippy watched the three forms of the bats hanging from the high ceiling, head down. Bull glanced at them twice and glared ahead again. His fists clenched.

"What a swell mess this turned out to be," he growled. "I'd like to lay my hands on the Heinie that hit me on the head."

Guards stopped them. The *leutnant* explained. The guards led the way into a concrete office, built on another end of the great cavern. A scar-faced, expressionless general was staring at them from across a desk. The leutnant was explaining the capture of Nippy and Bull.

"One of them should be the spy we are after, G-8," the *leutnant* said, more hopefully than convincingly.

"*Ach,*" the general spat. "I have a description of the size of G-8. That one—" pointing to Bull—"is much too big. And the other—" he glared at Nippy through his monocle—"is too small."

"But they are the assistants of G-8, *Excellenz,*" the *leutnant* insisted. "We have a guard at their planes."

Bull and Nippy both grew rigid.

"They are the planes that flew last night with G-8 and his Spad. Numbers 7 and 13, *Excellenz,*" the *leutnant* finished.

The general turned and glared at the two before him.

"Where is G-8, the master spy?" he demanded.

Bull shrugged and barked his answer.

"Never heard of him!"

Nippy opened his mouth. A *Kapitan* rushed into the room at that moment, highly excited, and snapped a salute to the general.

"We have just discovered the body of *Kapitan* Schlosser, your special messenger, among the rocks outside the island entrance," he announced.

General Ludenheim whirled on him.

"Impossible," he boomed. "*Kapitan* Schlosser was here not over an hour ago. I told him to stay about, as I would give him orders when I needed him again."

"*Ja,*" cut in the *Kapitan*. "But there can not be two *Kapitan* Schlossers, *Excellenz.*"

"Two?" boomed the general, leaping to his feet. "*Gott im Himmel.*"

He whirled and faced Bull and Nippy. He placed a trembling hand on each shoulder and tried to shake them.

"Speak. Where is G-8?"

No answer. He pushed them away, and fell to pacing the floor. Stopped before the *Kapitan* who had brought him the news of the discovered body. Glared at him.

"You are sure this body you have found is that of *Kapitan* Schlosser?" he demanded.

"*Jawohl, Excellenz.* He was my best friend. I could not be wrong."

General Ludenheim stepped back. His fists opened and closed.

"*Gott,* I remember now. Schlosser this time looked a little thinner. I thought it was the light."

He went into a tantrum of rage. He bellowed to his entire staff. He paced the floor while he talked.

"Fools, all of you. To be taken in by this spy, G-8. I am sure of it. No one else could do such a thing. Find the man who says he is *Kapitan* Schlosser and you will have the master spy of America. You will have G-8."

He beat his fist on his desk top like a madman.

"Find him, I tell you, or we are lost. Shoot him down in his tracks. Kill him. Put him out of the way. Gott, is it not enough to fight half the nations of the world, without having to be tricked by a *verdammt* spy like G-8?"

He sank into his desk chair, exhausted. His hands opened and closed. He waved toward the gaping Germans in the room.

"Ach. Heraus mit! Never come back until you have found G-8."

CHAPTER 16
"FIND G-8!"

G-8'S HEAD was spinning dizzily as he heard *Kapitan* Muzzen tell of the trap that was about to be laid for himself and Nippy and Bull. Muzzen was pointing to the bats again. His face was turned and he could not see the sudden change of expression flash across the face of the master spy.

With an effort, G-8 forced himself to calm once more. He even found he could laugh.

"Das ist gut," he said. "To trap G-8 and his assistants that way. *Ja.* That will be very good. And after you have caught G-8 and his men they will be killed? *Ja?"*

Kapitan Muzzen shrugged.

"*Jawohl*. Would we be foolish enough to once hold G-8 a prisoner and give him any chance of escape again? The most dangerous spy in the whole war?"

G-8 was making a mental map of the interior of the great cave of the bats. He changed the subject.

"But you have not told me how these giant bat machines work. How they are released and put into the air."

Muzzen nodded.

"*Ach, ja.* I had forgotten in talking about the plan to capture G-8 and his men."

He pointed toward the ceiling where a great cable looped. His hand swung to a giant boom of steel with the other end of the looped cable fastened to the end.

"Look," he went on. "When we open the door, that great rock slab you see which is swung open by electricity, this steel arm runs out, too. And when it runs out it tightens the cable on which the bat machines hang. Then one by one we shoot the bats out on the cable. Their motors are started before that, of course. And when we shoot them out on the cable they go with such force that they continue to fly straight on. The motors with the new mufflers sound like the fluttering of great wings. *Ja.* Is it not clever, Karl?"

"*Ach,* clever. *Jawohl. Jawohl,* Fritz," G-8 enthused. "But tell me, how does it work when the bats come back?"

Muzzen grinned.

"*Das ist* very simple," he explained. "When the bats land, one by one, they land on that rocky flat before the mountain which

THE BAT STAFFEL

I have told you about. At that time we let out the cable so that it lays on the ground."

He pointed to the bats hanging, heads downward, above.

"You see, their wings are folded automatically and they appear to be hanging by their engines that look in the night like their feet at the back edges of their wings. But there are hooks that extend beyond their propellers and which drag on the ground when they land. Instantly, when the hook catches in the cable, the cable is tightened, and the bat machine is snapped up, the wings fold automatically and they are shot through the door and hung out of the way high overhead. We land a single bat machine in less than ten seconds.

"*Ja?*" exclaimed G-8. "Wonderful."

"And all the invention of the great *doktor*, the great brain, *Herr Doktor* Krueger," grinned Muzzen proudly.

"*Ja,*" agreed G-8. "The clever one. He is a genius. But you must have to be very cautious about this gas that we have no masks to protect us from."

Muzzen nodded seriously.

"That I worry much about," he admitted. "It is my main job, to be in charge of that." He pointed to tanks along the wall. Great tanks with valves on their tops. "If ever even one of those should explode we would all be killed inside this trap. *Jawohl.* It would be horrible."

He pointed above the tanks.

"You see, up there are the blowers and ventilators that force fresh air through the tunnel from this end. The fresh air goes all the way through to the other end of the tunnel back in

G-8 AND HIS BATTLE ACES

Germany. I have argued with the engineers. That is the only mistake, I think, the *Herr Doktor* has made in his plans."

G-8 laughed.

"But you are foolish to be afraid," he said. "How could those strong tanks blow up in here? How could they blow up anywhere, *Herr Kapitan?*"

Muzzen shrugged.

"I suppose you are right," he admitted, "but they make me very nervous. Perhaps it is because I have been down here underground for several days without seeing the sunlight once."

G-8 nodded. "That is likely the reason."

"You will excuse me," said Muzzen. "I must see about having the bat machines loaded with their tanks of gas for tonight." He glanced at his wrist watch. "It is past time now. I did not realize."

He turned. G-8 smiled.

"And I must go back near the office of his *Excellenz*. He may want to send me on another mission with secret orders. I would like very much to fly one of those bat machines. It would be good fun to fly over France in the moonlight and drop the poison gas, *nicht wahr?* But we shall see—later."

"*Jawohl.* Good sport. Hunting on a big scale. Winning the war for the Vaterland. What do a few thousand French matter? I am glad to see you getting sensible, Karl."

"Perhaps then I shall be back later if I do not have a special job to perform," G-8 called.

HE LEFT then and strode down the great cave, past the office of his *Excellenz,* General Ludenheim. He passed with

THE BAT STAFFEL

plenty of room to spare, out of sight of the guards, for he wanted time to think. A special outside mission tonight wasn't in his present scheme of things. He must be on hand when the bats flew out. He must have time to develop some plan to end this devilish raid before more French people were killed.

He noticed that the troops were growing restless—tense. He recalled the words of Ludenheim's message to von Kuhl. According to that message, the fifty thousand German troops in the tunnel would move out over France as soon as the deadly gas had been spread and the wind had had time to sweep the area free again.

That would probably be about dawn.

Already orders must have been given, for the air was tense with excitement. And still there seemed to be a spirit everywhere of light-heartedness. A feeling of assurance. Soldiers talked. *Offiziers* joked among themselves as they waited.

Soon the war would be over. Germany would win. And once winning from the Allies, they would move over the rest of the world—bat's breath sweeping away all opposition before them.

For one, two hours G-8 walked and listened and saluted until his arm ached. He had passed through the tunnel and had entered the old mine. More soldiers were moving here—moving past constantly now. The time was drawing nearer.

He smiled to himself as he thought of that special message to von Kuhl. The changing of a P to an A would make all the difference in the world to one hundred thousand Germans—if his plan worked. The last troops would enter that tunnel at the north end at about one in the morning.

He walked through the great, low-ceilinged, abandoned mine and entered the passage which led to the narrow tunnel under the Rhine River.

Never once did G-8 dream that there was a trap about to be set for him. Far ahead he saw the guards who stood at the entrance, where the narrow passage from the island joined the main tunnel. He smiled as he recalled the password. How the sergeant there had laughed when he put the password into a sentence.

An *offizier*, a *Kapitan*, dived through the passage from the small tunnel. G-8 watched him, saw him stop for an instant, highly excited. He spoke briefly to the sergeant, then broke into a run toward the mine.

Instinctively, G-8 stepped behind a nearby post and turned his head. The man raced on without noticing him.

G-8 stepped from behind the post and watched him until his running form was out of sight around a bend in the passage. He began formulating his desperate plan as he strolled back.

He would be in the cave of the bats when the machines were released. At the moment when the door opened to allow the first one to leave, he would leap for the gas tank valves on the wall. Holding his breath, he would open wide as many valves as he could.

Then he would close the great rock door with the control switch and try to dive through before it would be too late.

The gas would do the rest. Germans would be taken by surprise. They wouldn't have time to open the doors and run. They wouldn't be able to think quickly enough to do anything

THE BAT STAFFEL

before the gas of their own making struck them dead and began its shrinking power. The ventilators would carry the gas on through the tunnel.

If only the bat machines didn't start their flight until those hundred thousand troops started entering the tunnel!

He moved on slowly, engrossed in his plans.

He had almost reached the old mine again when suddenly he heard the sound of running feet from behind. Turning in the shadow of a pillar he glanced back. The sergeant was running toward him!

G-8'S HAND moved to his Luger. Quickly he loosened it, so that it could be pulled from the holster easily. Then he turned to face the approaching German.

"You are *Kapitan* Schlosser?" the sergeant demanded excitedly.

G-8 hesitated for only an instant.

"*Ja.* I am. *Was ist?*"

The Luger of the sergeant came up and leveled at G-8's middle.

"*Ach.* You are under arrest," he barked. "Come!"

G-8 tensed. Slowly his hands rose a little. Then he laughed.

"But surely," he said, "there must be some mistake. Of course I am *Kapitan* Shiller, but what could you want with me?"

"Shiller?" the sergeant blinked and stared harder at G-8. "*Kapitan* Shiller? But you look like—you are *Kapitan* Schlosser."

G-8 laughed derisively then.

"*Ach, nein,*" he insisted. "Shiller. I said yes. I thought you asked

G-8 AND HIS BATTLE ACES

me if I was *Kapitan* Shiller. That is my name. *Ach*, you should learn to *macht Deutsches sprechen als besser*, Sergeant. Away and do not bother me. Who is it you want to arrest?"

The sergeant hesitated. He couldn't seem to make up his mind. His eyes narrowed as he stared at the cleverly made-up face of G-8. An angry growl came from his throat.

"*Verdammt,*" he shouted. "You are the man who is impersonating *Kapitan* Schlosser. Put up your hands."

Cornered! G-8 moved with astonishing speed. He leaped sidewise, darted behind the post.

Blam! The Luger in the sergeant's hand blasted. The walls of the passage echoed, caused the ears of G-8 to ring. It seemed the vibration would cave in the sides.

Blam! Blam! Two other shots rang out and reverberated through the underground passages. Those shots came from the Luger that had appeared abruptly in the hand of G-8. He was shooting around the post. Flame and steel snorted from his Luger.

The sergeant grunted. Bent double. His head wobbled on his sagging shoulders. Down—down he slumped, until he was a twitching heap of flesh and bone on the hard floor.

G-8 was away, then, like a frightened rabbit. The sound of heavy boots echoed through the vaults. The shots had drawn other Germans!

G-8 dived for the darker recesses of the passage, broke through the concrete tunnel and turned into the wider expanse of the old mine. Two men blocked his way.

THE BAT STAFFEL

His Luger blasted four times and they toppled over, cursing and groaning.

Without stopping, he plunged on toward the darker portion of the mine. It must have walls where he would be trapped. He felt the end was coming. Still he never once thought of giving up.

He slipped another clip into his Luger. Raced on and on. Came to a dark corner and crouched there. Running feet were pounding after him. They stopped suddenly. The Boches were growing cautious.

As he crouched there, he wondered how Nippy and Bull were making out. There had been a trap set for them. Had it worked? Forgetting his own danger for the instant, he breathed a prayer for his recently chosen pals.

He shifted his gaze. A close-cropped head peered around the edge of a great post that helped support the ceiling of the mine.

G-8 slunk farther back into his corner. Lay motionless. So long as no light was flashed in his direction, he was safe. If there were only some hole or depression in the floor to hide in. But there was none.

Then came the light he had hoped would not come. And yet he had been sure that it would. The Germans would hunt him down to the death. There could be no mistaking their hatred for him—the man who had blasted plans and hopes with seeming ease.

A FLASHLIGHT beam slashed the gloom. G-8 was down as flat as he could get on the floor behind a post. But the post was not wide enough to cover him entirely. He heard stealthy footsteps moving toward his hiding place.

He moved just a little, shifted so that he could peer around the edge of the post.

Luger in hand, a big German was creeping up on him. Too close for comfort.

Blam! G-8's Luger leaped and boomed. The German clutched his middle and toppled.

*Instan*tly, G-8 was on his feet. As he ran it seemed that every pillar and post gave up a German soldier.

Crack! Crack! Crack!

Steel rained all about him. It spattered against the wall beside him. A slug slashed through his sleeve and gashed his arm. He plunged on. Lights were trying to pick him up, but the darkness hid him still so that the shots did not come true.

He fired his Luger again and again. Knocked Germans kicking. Taught them to be more cautious. They were in the light and he was running in the dark, except as beams from hand torches cracked the black about him.

He came to a dead end suddenly. The wall of the mine turned abruptly. Left him in a pocket in the corner. He leaped out along the wall that ran at right angles. Germans came running and firing straight ahead. A shout of triumph came from fifty guttural throats.

Trapped!

G-8 whirled and crouched. His Luger was almost too hot to hold. It was already scorching his hand. He slipped another clip into the gun and crouched behind a post.

THE BAT STAFFEL

"O.K.," he barked. "You want it. Come and get it. And may the Good Lord have mercy on your souls—if you've got any."

Blam! Crack! Boom!

Slugs ripped the wooded side of the post. Plopped into the wood. Plunked against the earth wall behind.

And for every shot that left that hot Luger in G-8's hand a German fell over and groaned in the throes of death.

Step by step German soldiers advanced. He couldn't hold out forever. Wood splintered in his face. He took aim and pulled again.

Blam! Something boomed and burst wide open before his eyes. Lights went out. A million flashes appeared before him—then silence and total darkness.

CHAPTER 17
G-8, PRISONER

THE FIRST realization that G-8 had of returning consciousness was a dull aching in his head, being made more painful by the guttural voices of men about him.

He moved his head. Rolled it to the other side to try to stop the pain.

"Ach," one voice exploded. "He lives. *Verdammt* G-8. He lives and—"

"—now we have to kill him all over again," another cut in with a harsh laugh.

G-8 relaxed. For the moment he wasn't sure but what death

would be rather welcome. The thought passed almost instantly and another took its place.

"Come," said a new voice. "We must take him to his *Excellenz*. Wake him up if you can, *Doktor*. Perhaps we can make him walk. We will not have to carry him. But we must hurry. It is almost time for the bat machines to leave and then we soldiers follow. We must be ready."

That meant that G-8 had been out for some time. It must be nearly midnight. Perhaps after. He hoped so. Desperately he clenched his teeth against the pain in his head and opened his eyes. Angry round faces stared down upon him. He was lying on a surgeon's table, and a man in white was bending over him.

"Just a bad knock on the head," the surgeon had concluded as G-8 opened his eyes and sat up.

G-8 put his hand to his head. A bandage was there, soaked near the temple with half dried blood. He glanced from one face to another. And then he did a strange thing. He smiled.

"Well," he said, "I guess that's that. Who am I supposed to be and where do we go from here?"

A *leutnant* seemed to take command.

"We know you are G-8, the *verdammt* spy," he said. "We will take you now to His *Excellenz*, General Ludenheim. After that—" the *leutnant* grinned as though he were about to mention something pleasant—"you will be shot."

G-8 shrugged.

"Why not shoot me now?" he ventured. "Why bother to take

THE BAT STAFFEL

me to a great general like His *Excellenz,* General Ludenheim? He is a very busy man. I know. I was special messenger for him."

The *leutnant* smiled.

"Ach. Perhaps you do not realize what a prize you are, *Herr* G-8. Already His *Excellenz* knows of your capture. We thought at first that you were dead. Then when we learned that you would live and that it was only a glancing blow on the head you had received, we informed His *Excellenz* of the fact and he ordered us to bring you to him."

G-8 nodded slowly. A smile played about his lips.

"I suppose your High Command wishes to have me held by the arms so that he can hurl taunts at me. Is that it, *Herr Leutnant?"*

The *leutnant's* face flushed angrily.

"His *Excellenz* does not have to keep you held. He is one general who is a good man with any weapon you might choose. Come. We go at once."

G-8 GOT to his feet a bit unsteadily. Heavily guarded, he strode from the room. Outside, he glanced about. They were in the great stone cave, near the office of General Ludenheim.

Guards presented arms at the door of the office. They stole curious, awed glances at the prisoner with the bandage about his head and the blood oozing through.

General Ludenheim was pacing the floor when they entered. He turned with a jerk and eyed G-8. For a long time he stared at the master spy. And even in the gaze of the great general there was awe and pride too.

G-8 noted that. Took stock of every move, every glance. For

some time they simply stood and eyed each other. Then G-8 smiled easily.

"Again we meet, general," he said, "but this time on more equal terms. I think."

"You admit that you are G-8, the great American spy?" Ludenheim demanded.

G-8 shrugged.

"Of course. Why deny it? I am not ashamed of it."

"Ashamed?" barked the general. "Gott, I should say not. Who would be ashamed of being so great a spy as you? But your admittance of your identity condemns you for certain to die as a spy. To die before the firing squad. You understand that, *Herr* G-8?"

G-8 nodded.

"Of course." He made a wry face. "But that way of dying, *Excellenz*. Is it necessary that I die before a firing squad?"

"And how else would you die?" demanded the general.

"There are many ways to die," G-8 laughed. "And it seems no more than fair that the one to die so abruptly should be allowed to pick his own way. His favorite way, perhaps."

Ludenheim glared at him for an instant.

"This is no time to joke, *Herr* G-8."

G-8 laughed harshly.

"You're telling me?" he said. "But listen. You say I must die, *nicht wahr*. And you say I should die before a firing squad. I do not like a firing squad. It would make me feel like a common criminal. Surely there should be some better, more fitting way for one so great to die."

THE BAT STAFFEL

He tried to swell his chest out to make his ego sound real.

"And if you do kill me, then what will you do? You will simply bury me, with a squad of guns shooting their second volley, over me that time—and you will proudly send back a note to the Allies telling them you have shot and killed their great spy."

"*Gott im Himmel!*" exploded General Ludenheim. "What would you have us do with you, stuff you and put you in a museum?"

G-8 laughed.

"Hardly that. I'm not worth that much, I'm afraid. But you might prove to the Allies that I was dead by sending my body back to them. You might even drop it from one of your bat planes."

The eyes of the general lighted.

G-8 didn't wait for him to answer. He raced on with his wild, insane plan.

"Wait. I have a better way. Instead of the firing squad, I will be carried over France in the first bat plane that leaves tonight. I will be tightly bound. What could be more fitting, a more heroic death, than to be pitched over the cockpit of that bat plane to land ten thousand feet down in the center of the Rue de la Paix in Paris?"

General Ludenheim stared at him in astonishment. He shook his head gravely.

"You are a very brave man, *Herr* G-8," he said, "or else you are insane. But your idea is not bad if I could be sure that your cleverness would not accomplish another escape for you."

G-8 grinned.

G-8 AND HIS BATTLE ACES

"You have great confidence in your soldiers, *Excellenz,* if you think that a man tightly bound and imprisoned in one of your bat planes could escape. Would you expect me to break strong ropes and step out on a cloud? But perhaps you are right. If you feel that your soldiers are weaklings, then don't take any chance."

Purple flushed the face of Ludenheim.

"That is an insult, *Herr* G-8. For it, you shall die as you propose," he flamed angrily. "You shall be tightly bound in one of the eye cockpits of the first bat machine to fly tonight. You shall be bound in such a way that you cannot escape. The pilot will only have to pull a rope and you will topple out of the cockpit and fall ten thousand feet to your death."

Ludenheim whirled and shouted his orders. G-8 glanced at his watch an instant before strong hands twisted his arms behind his back to be tied.

Twelve-thirty! His heart leaped. He might be in time yet. If his plan worked and there were no hitches, he would be. The hundred thousand men would be moving in at the north end of the tunnel in half an hour.

HE WINCED and groaned as they jerked tight ropes into his flesh. He spread his muscles without seeming to strain. The ropes tightened. Strong hands pulled on them. His hands were fastened by ropes from his neck and his feet.

Four husky Germans picked him up and carried him down the cave. Already the sound of motors echoed through the vaulted walls. Mercedes motors warming.

Men worked on scaffolds about the three hanging bat ma-

THE BAT STAFFEL

chines. Surprising what a small amount of space those planes took up, hanging to the ceiling with their wings folded.

Guards were all about him. The curious came to glance at him and then moved away. Up, up he was carried on a long ladder. Then along one of the scaffolds to the first bat machine.

Two cockpits were close together in the head of the machine. Two cockpits which resembled the eyes of the bat. Roughly, they lowered him into the right-hand one.

They tied him half leaning out, fastened to the plane by a slip knot on the rope. The other end of the rope would be in the hands of the pilot in the opposite cockpit about three feet away. One pull and G-8 would topple over and hurl to his death.

A giant, round-headed, scar-faced German pilot stepped to the other cockpit. He grinned at G-8.

"I have a passenger, ja? And I have my orders," he chuckled. "To be delivered in the Rue de la Paix in one hour. This is an honor, *Herr* G-8. And a pleasure."

He settled into his seat. The motors roared. There came a shouted signal. G-8 shot a glance at the wall of stone. It was moving outward. The great steel boom was running out after and the cable was tightening.

Then with a roar, like the flutter of giant wings, the bat plane slithered down the cable. The wings snapped open the minute the doorway was passed. And the giant man-made bat was in flight.

CHAPTER 18
THE DEATH PATROL

NIPPY WESTON and Bull Martin turned a shade paler as they stood in the office of His *Excellenz* General Ludenheim, and heard that high officer proclaim that G-8 should die.

The realization flashed over each at the same time that their leader, G-8, was in a trap. A trap that would spring about him without his suspecting it.

Offiziers and men were hurrying out of the office before the wild, glaring eyes of their commandant. Two guards jabbed Nippy and Bull in the backs with Lugers and ordered them to march.

Interest was no longer centered on the two Yanks; it had switched to G-8 and his capture.

The two strode from the office, hurried by their guards. Where before there had been a dozen guards about them with drawn guns, not to mention several *offiziers,* now there were but two guards left to hold them.

One of the guards gave the order to halt. Both stopped. Bull turned and faced his captor.

"Well, where do we go from here, Heinie?" he demanded.

He spoke in his best German. The guard glanced about speculatively and shrugged.

"Ich weis nicht," he said. "I know not."

Nippy grinned.

THE BAT STAFFEL

"Go ahead. Run away and start looking for G-8, fella. See if we care."

The guard seemed not to notice him. He saluted an *offizier* who was passing.

"These two prisoners we have, *Herr Leutnant*," he said. "They are not spies like their leader. They are only prisoners of war. But we have no prison camp except just outside the other end of the tunnel. Orders are for no man to leave the tunnel. What shall we do with these two?"

The *offizier* stared from Nippy to Bull. He glanced about the rear end of the cave of the bats, then jerked his head in that direction.

"These two, it does not matter," he said. "We are after G-8. Tie them up, and one of you watch them. They are not dangerous."

Bull flushed. Stepped forward and was forced back at the point of the Luger.

"That's an insult," he boomed. "I resent that."

But his words came in English.

"Was sagen sie?" the *offizier* demanded.

Nippy jabbed Bull in the ribs with his elbow.

"He says it's past his bed time. He wants to go to sleep," Nippy explained in fair German, trying not to laugh.

"Dummkopf!" sputtered the *offizier*. "Take them away. Over there out of the way. The Bats will be going out before long. And then when they return all of us will get out of this *verdammt* hole in the ground. It doesn't matter much what happens

to these two. We will have all of France in twenty-four hours if the *verdammt* spy, G-8, is discovered and put out of the way."

The guard who had acted as spokesman handed the other his Luger. With a gun in each hand, the lone guard ordered Bull and Nippy to march to the darker corner of the cavern, away from the activity.

The other guard returned at almost the same time they reached the point in the cavern. He carried a coil of wire in his hand. Heavy wire, it was, in a long strand, wound in a series of loops.

"Ach, there is no rope here. We must bind them up with this wire, Hans," he said. "You hold them with your gun and I will do the tying up, *Ja?"*

Bull growled. Nippy poked him in the ribs. He winked at his big friend as their hands were being bound with the wire. Then their feet were tied and they were forced to lay down on the damp, rocky floor of the cave.

A loop of wire was run from the foot bindings to the hands. The guards surveyed their work with satisfaction.

"Hans," said the first, "I go back to my work. You stay here and guard these two. And do not fall asleep. I will return at midnight and take your place. *Nicht wahr?"*

Hans nodded. The other went away. From their position on the damp stone floor Bull and Nippy could see little. Three hours dragged by.

NIPPY ROLLED close to Bull. The guard was standing sidewise to them with his back against a stone column. Now

THE BAT STAFFEL

and then at long intervals he glanced at them. His Luger was back in its holster.

"Can you move at all?" Nippy hissed. "Any chance of getting out of this mess, slipping the halter, I mean?"

Bull turned his head and glared at him.

"And if we do, then what?"

"Got a hunch," Nippy hissed back in his ear. "Try. See what you can do."

Bull strained. He moved so that his back was turned to Nippy's back. That would let Nippy's hands work on the wire that held his arms.

The guard turned his head toward them. Both Nippy and Bull stopped. The guard looked away again, engrossed in watching preparations for the bat machines' departure.

Again Nippy began to work at the wire. His fingers were getting sore. He slashed one. Worked on.

"Coming," hissed Bull as he strained.

The guard turned and glanced at them in another fifteen minutes. They stopped work. Lay motionless. The guard looked away.

"Got any idea what time it is?" That from Nippy.

"No. Can't see my wrist watch. Here I'll roll over. Take a look."

Nippy looked. "Half-past eleven," he whispered. "Listen. This other guard will be back any time now. He might take it into his head to make sure we're still tied up when he comes on. Let's get things a little looser and then wait for him."

"Yeah?" hissed Bull. "Then what? I suppose all we got to do

is get up and walk out of here. Don't forget we're dressed in the good old Yankee uniform. We'll be about as prominent with all these Heinies as a sore thumb at a piano recital."

"Forget it," Nippy pleaded. "I got a hunch, I tell you. And if there's any justice, it'll work. Remember this other guy said something about the bat machines would be going out shortly? Well, we go out right after the first of those, see?"

Bull shook his head, tugged at the wire that held his wrists and growled something about fool ideas.

"I didn't think you'd get it," Nippy chirped still in a whisper. "Well, you'll see. Pipe down now."

Minutes passed. Fifteen. Twenty minutes. A figure came from the more brightly lighted part of the cavern. Hans pushed himself away from the pillar and went to meet his friend.

"How goes it, Hans?" the other asked.

"Nothing has happened." He yawned. "I am glad you have come. I was almost asleep standing up."

"Come," said the other. "We see first are they still tightly tied up yet."

A flashlight flashed on the wires. Nippy tensed. He glanced over his shoulder. Yes, Bull had taken his advice. His hands were still bound at the wrists.

"Still tied up, Hans," said the newcomer. "You can go now. I take care of them."

The new guard stood over against the same stone column that his friend Hans had held up. He also watched the activity about the more brightly lighted part of the cave. Now and then he turned and shot a glance at the two figures on the floor.

THE BAT STAFFEL

Once more Nippy worked feverishly at the wires that bound Bull's wrists. Bull tugged and strained. The wire was separating. The guard looked over. They stopped. He turned away.

Bull's hands came free. Instantly, he twisted on the wire about Nippy's wrists. A half minute and that came free. They worked at their legs. Cursed the guard for looking again. He missed anything suspicious about their movements.

Their feet were free now. Nippy laid a restraining hand on Bull's arm.

"Listen," he hissed. "I can move without making as much noise as you. You lie down. Turn over. Your body is bigger than mine. He will think he is seeing both of us if he looks while I am gone."

Bull nodded and turned over.

"Wait until he looks this way once more."

ONE, TWO minutes. The guard turned and glanced at them. They were lying as they had been before. The guard turned again to look the other way.

"So long," whispered Nippy.

He felt the pressure of the big hand on his arm.

"Good luck." Bull hissed back.

Nippy crept out across the stone floor. He was making good time. Noiseless time. Step after step. He headed for the back of the pillar.

He froze in a shadow as the guard turned. But it was only a fleeting glance, and the Boche turned quickly again to watch what was going on in the larger part of the great cave.

Step by step, Nippy drew closer to him. He was directly

behind the guard now. Behind the stone pillar. He could see the Luger in its holster. His hand reached for it. Fingers touched the butt.

Swiftly, he clutched and pulled.

Out came the Luger. The guard felt the stroke and whirled. He stared into the grinning face of Nippy Weston.

Nippy spoke in German.

"One peep out of you and you die, Heinie," he said. "Move this way. Quick."

The German moved to raise his hands. His face went white with fear. Nippy poked the gun in his ribs.

"Put down your hands," he ordered. "Get going. Do as I say and you're not going to get hurt."

The German seemed to come out of his trance then. He stepped toward the spot where the two had been lying. Bull leaped to his feet.

"Tie him up," Nippy hissed. "And I mean, tie him. We'll gag him to make sure he doesn't yell his fool head off."

The former guard was too frightened to argue, to say anything. His eyes seemed held by that Luger in Nippy's hand. Bull had the German's feet and hands tied. The German winced with the pain of the tight wires, but dared not utter a sound.

Nippy tore out one of the tails of his shirt, stuffed it into the Boche's mouth and he bound it in firmly with wire. Together they made a last inspection of their prisoner.

"Hog-tied, if I ever saw such a thing," Bull grinned.

"Right. Let's go," Nippy said.

"Where?"

THE BAT STAFFEL

Nippy coiled the wire that had been employed in binding him. With that in one hand and the Luger in the other he jerked his head to Bull to follow and moved a little nearer the lighted part of the cave.

The section where they had been was low-ceilinged. It seemed waste space. All the activity was out beyond, a hundred yards or more distant.

They could see more plainly now. Hundreds of soldiers were stationed throughout the great high-vaulted cavern. They saw the three bats hanging from the ceiling, men working on the scaffolds about them.

Suddenly, Nippy clutched Bull's arm and stopped him. He pointed with the coil toward a moving group of men.

"Look," he said. "Something funny there. They're carrying something or somebody."

Side by side, they crouched in the shadow of a stone pillar. Bull frowned.

"Can't figure that one out. Why would they be carrying anybody to one of those machines? Look. They're taking him up that ladder to the scaffold and the bat machines."

They watched, stared until it seemed that their eyes would pop out. But now that the men carrying their burden had reached a scaffold, they could not see the burden that they carried at all, as the hanging bat was turned with that side away from them.

Nippy's gaze shifted to other parts of the cave. Near the great stone door the ceiling sloped so that at one point at the left a man could hardly stand erect.

"Come on," he hissed.

Leading Bull along the edge of the cave, they crept through the darker recesses. Cases of supplies were piled in front of that low-ceiling section.

They reached it just as a roaring flutter beat the air.

"Look!" Bull was pointing from their new position behind the supply boxes at the side. "Look. See where the engines are? There on the tail end of the wings hooked to the middle joint. Two pushers on each of the three crates and—"

He clutched Nippy's arm until the little Yank winced with pain.

"See. Just as I guessed. Those eyes. The eyes of the things are the cockpits. If we make a direct hit in either or both of them we'll get the guys who fly the crates. That'll be the end of that story."

Nippy grinned in the semi-darkness.

"Your idea, eh?" he said.

Bull shrugged.

"Well, what's the difference so long as we get 'em?"

"Check," said Nippy. "Now, here's my plan."

AS HE talked, he straightened out the wire. Producing a large piece of cheese cloth from under his blouse, he bent the wire, made loops and folded the cloth in a strange way. Bull frowned as he looked on.

"Holy Herring," he muttered. "More ghosts?"

"Right. Maybe this'll get us out. Here's the dope. I'll attract attention with this thing when the door opens. Whenever

THE BAT STAFFEL

Heinie turns to see what's going on, that's the time we make a hop, skip and jump for the door. Get it?"

Bull grinned.

"Do I get it? That's a honey. And if they try to stop us, watch me bowl 'em—"

Nippy laid a hand on his arm and pointed. The pilot of the first bat machine had taken his seat. They could see a figure plainly in the other cockpit. Another German *offizier*. Something strange about him—

The roaring, fluttery sound increased. A clanking noise sounded near at hand. The great stone door was opening, swinging out. A steel arm with attached cable was swinging through the door. Fifty odd Germans crowded about the opening. The time for a break wasn't ripe yet.

The bat machine shot out across the cable. The giant wings unfolded as though by magic. With a scream, the machine shot into the air and disappeared into the night.

Suddenly another sound filled the cavern. A weird, wailing sound that seemed to come from the doorway.

Germans turned. Heads craned. Eyes popped. Something white and strange was drifting in on the night breeze that swept in through the open door. The door was closing but the thing was already inside! The sound increased to a bloodcurdling scream. The thing, white and flapping and glowing, seemed to be making the sound. The apparition settled. Germans leaped away from it.

"Now!" hissed Nippy.

Bull leaped from behind the cases. Nippy was at his heels,

G-8 AND HIS BATTLE ACES

Luger in hand. Staring eyes were upon the settling white thing as it came down slowly.

Suddenly, eyes turned caught by the swift movement of the fleeing pair. And the Yank's swift flight was vitally necessary, for at that very moment the door was half closed and they were still a hundred feet from it, running for their lives.

Germans in front prepared to stop them. Guns barked from behind. Nippy ran like a wild thing, shooting as he ran.

But Bull Martin, All American Half two years before, was going into action in his own way.

His head was down. One hundred and ninety pounds of muscle, hard as rock, was charging with the speed of a bullet straight through that mass of Germans.

A challenging bellow came from Bull's throat.

"Let's goooo! Follow your interference, Nippy!"

Germans ahead of them seemed either so awed by that charge or so astonished by the sudden appearance of the two odd-sized Yanks that they forgot they had guns. The challenge seemed to be to stop this mad, plunging hellion with their hands. To play a game rather than resort to war.

Nippy was following his interference as though he and Bull were one and the same unit.

Germans tried to stop that charge. They sprawled. Twice Bull straight-armed two giant Germans and sent them spinning out of the way, end over end.

The doors were closing. Only ten feet of space left.

Two more Germans crouched before them and freedom.

THE BAT STAFFEL

Wam! Bull hit that line of the enemy like a charging rhino. The two huge Germans scattered, one flying in either direction.

Nippy came on at his heels.

The door was within five feet of closing when they shot through. There was a clanking and grating sound as the portal shut.

The two Yanks ran headlong toward the place where they had left their planes. No telling if they were there still or not. And if they were there, they would likely be under guard.

Almost instantly, the door of stone opened again. Light sprayed out, full onto Nippy and Bull, who were running wildly across the level plateau.

Shouts came from far behind.

"If our ships are gone, we're sunk," Bull panted.

"Yeah. And where would they go? They wouldn't fly them away this soon," argued Nippy, between gasps for breath as he ran. "They think they're going to take the whole of France in twenty-four hours. Why should they worry about a couple of Spads? Just the same, we'll go slow from now on. Probably they'll have a—"

He stopped short and stared. He crouched, pulled Bull down beside him and pointed across the rocky level in the moonlight. A guard, stood before their planes. He held a rifle leveled at them. He shouted a command.

NIPPY DROPPED flat and lifted his Luger. He took careful aim. Pulled three times.

Crack! The rifle of the guard blasted at the same instant. A slug whistled over their heads.

The guard toppled over, fell flat on his face and lay still.

Bull and Nippy leaped to their feet and ran on. Props spun. Nippy's Hisso was balky. Germans were coming nearer and nearer. Shooting as they came now. With a roar, Nippy's Hisso caught, too. He leaped to his cockpit.

Together they hit the throttles. No time to wait for warming motors. Straight at those running Germans, they charged. The tails of the two ships came up. Vickers steel sprayed Germans. They fell and lay still.

Out across the moonlit space the Spads roared. They grew light and lifted.

As though controlled by one hand, they turned west, in the direction they were sure the bat machine had taken.

Minutes of tense flying. Of looking. Watching all over the moonlit heavens for that weird Bat form that flew so slowly and so surely.

Nippy spotted it first. He veered toward Bull. Bull could make out his pointing in the dim light. His teeth clenched.

Together they romped down on the bat plane, one from each side. Then suddenly, Bull yanked on the stick and shot his Spad high into the air ahead of the slower moving monster.

His hand dove into the side of his cockpit and came out with a flare. He hurled it overboard, kicked over and roared down.

"You're going to get it now and in plenty of light," he rasped through clenched teeth. "Right in the eye."

Down, down. He pressed his guns for a warning burst. Vickers spoke in instant answer.

He had circled from above. Was coming in now almost di-

THE BAT STAFFEL

rectly at the bat plane. He thought the head moved, but he couldn't be sure. Perhaps when the plane swerved slightly it appeared as though the head turned a little.

But the eyes were what he was interested in. He could see them both plainly in the light of the flare. Two eyes close together. Two cockpits, they were—Bull Martin knew that now. But he didn't know or dream who the passenger in that one cockpit was.

He only knew that a German-clad figure in one cockpit was half out over the edge—knew that, therefore, he was a better shot for the first crack than the other.

"Here you go, number one," he rasped.

He plunged down, glared and caught the German-clad figure that was G-8 directly in the cross wires of his sights!

CHAPTER 19
FIGHT OF THE BATS

HARDLY TEN seconds after G-8 had been tied into the cockpit of the great bat plane, he was tugging and straining at the ropes that bound his wrists. His legs were beyond hope—at least until he could get his hands free—if ever.

The bat plane shot across the catapult cable, flashed through the opened stone doorway. The wings unfolded automatically and the machine was in flight.

Darkness settled about them as they climbed. Dimly he could see the pilot in the other cockpit. The Boche looked over and grinned.

"Enjoy your last ride while you can, *Mein Herr*," he advised.

A brutal laugh came from his thick throat. The motors throbbed behind, with the mufflers making their sound resemble the flutter of giant wings.

G-8 grinned back.

"Nice night for it, anyway," he observed.

Carefully, cautiously, he strained. He must be careful not to let the pilot see him working at his bindings. Must take care not to irritate his wrists so that they would swell.

Now that he relaxed his muscles the ropes about his wrists were looser. There would be plenty of time to work his hands free before reaching Paris and the Rue de la Paix. He smiled to himself at the thought. That had been a happy brain child— that idea of demanding a fitting death.

He stared up at the moon. It was full and riding high in the sky. He moved a little to get more comfortable. His position was cramped. He was tied half out of the cockpit with his feet inside, so that the edge of the cockpit cut into his stomach. Well, it wouldn't be long. His hands were growing looser all of the time. Turning his head, he stared back at the face of the mountain. The thought of Nippy and Bull had troubled him much. A trap had been laid for them. Had they been caught? He had no way of knowing. If they were held prisoner inside that cave—there was a possibility of it—then his plans would have to wait. Never would he take a chance of killing them. As he glanced back he saw the stone door open. He hadn't noticed it close, but it must have done so after they had left—and was just opening again.

THE BAT STAFFEL

Then he grew suddenly rigid. Something—a plane—had flashed past that open door. He could see it against the light.

A split second later another plane flashed past the opening. G-8 turned. He saw the eyes of the big pilot fixed upon him across the stretch that separated their two strange cockpits. G-8 relaxed. The pilot stared ahead again.

Now G-8 worked more frantically than ever at the ropes about his wrists. Slipping, slipping. But he couldn't know of the danger that was to come. Didn't know, in fact, until two Spads roared above the giant bat plane and a flare burst out in brilliance high above.

One Spad circled and plunged down. The other came on from behind. Straight as an arrow that one Spad dove.

A stream of white tracers lashed down at him. He could see them fluffing brightly in the light of the flare. The Spad was still out of range. That was a warming burst. A warning that more was coming.

Even from that distance and by the light of the falling magnesium flare he could distinguish the big head and shoulders of the pilot. That would be Bull Martin. And the other, of course, that would be Nippy Weston. They hadn't been trapped. Or if they had, they had escaped.

G-8 worked like mad at the ropes now. Nearer and nearer came that deadly Spad. The warming burst was over. The next shot would be to kill. Bull Martin had flawless aim.

As G-8 hung there fighting to get his hands free he suddenly felt lost. An angry growl came from the German pilot. In the light of the flare he had seen G-8 freeing his hands.

G-8 AND HIS BATTLE ACES

"One more move and you die!" the voice bellowed.

EVERYTHING SEEMED to happen so quickly. G-8 got his hands free as the pilot finished speaking. He brought them up. Waved wildly at Bull who was coming head-on. But even as he did so, he realized that the blood-soaked bandage hid his face. Realized, too, that he had changed his make-up since Bull had seen him last. But perhaps Bull would see his waving. Would guess that something was wrong.

Suddenly, he remembered that under the coat of his German uniform he wore his U.S. Army shirt. Buttons flew. His hand ripped open the uniform coat. Showed the crossed propeller and wings, the insignia of the U.S. Air Service. And beside it the U.S.A. letters on the turned-in collar.

Bull came on. G-8 gasped. Was the man blind? Couldn't he see? Couldn't he understand?

Then something else happened. G-8 suddenly felt himself slipping. He was falling. Tipping out of the cockpit. The pilot had held to his threat—had pulled the slip knot.

Frantically he clutched the sides of the cockpit for support. Bull hurled closer.

Tac-tac-tac!

G-8 couldn't see that diving Spad now. He was almost upside down, tumbling out with his feet tied together.

Tac-tac-tac! Tac-tac-tac!

Again that short burst and then another burst from another angle. That would be Nippy cutting in from the side. G-8 was fighting as he had never fought before. A bullet would end it all. His hold would slip and he would go to his death.

THE BAT STAFFEL

The bat plane lurched. He slipped, fought desperately to hold on. Down, down the bat plane hurled.

G-8 heaved. His finger nails bit into the edge of the cockpit. Left marks there. With a mighty effort he succeeded against the whipping wind and the lurching of the plane.

He was pulling himself back into the cockpit. Somehow he felt that he should have bullets in him. He stared about for a split second. The moon was straight behind him. That meant the bat ship was in a dive for the earth.

Whirling, he stared across at the Boche pilot. He was slumped over his controls; the stick was jammed ahead against the instrument board. The pilot was dead.

Two Spads roared in close as the bat plane continued to hurl down.

G-8 leaped across the space between the two cockpits. The German was very heavy and anyway the small cockpit was cramped for two. But with a heave, G-8 jerked the pilot's body off the stick. He pulled the stick back. The lumbering bat plane took her time, but finally came out of the death dive.

A moment later he had the ship flying level again. With one hand he unstrapped the helmet and goggles from the German's chin, took it off and slipped it on his own head over the bandage.

Heaving the Boche's body out of the cockpit—and dropping it over the side—while he kept the plane on an even wing took all of his strength and skill. But he made it. He settled into the cockpit at last, placed his feet on the controls. Took a long breath.

The two Spads circled above. The flare had burned out. But

now another burst just ahead as Spad number 13, zoomed and dropped it.

G-8 stood up in the cockpit and waved in the light. He waved the Spads closer.

While they came down, almost touching wings with the giant bat plane, he studied his controls and instruments. They were arranged much the same as those of a Fokker D-7. He pulled back on the throttle, stuck the nose into a gentle glide.

Bull came down behind. G-8 turned, grinned and waved. Bull's motor was turning over slowly. And behind him came Nippy, with his motor idling also.

Half standing, G-8 began to shout across as Bull, with a faster gliding plane, crept by.

"Go back and get other bats. Two more. Shoot in cockpits." **BULL NODDED** and waved. Nippy's Spad slithered down. Only the *ca-plunk-a-plunk* of the motors bothered the speaking.

G-8 raised his voice and repeated the order. Nippy grinned and kicked over.

G-8 then turned the great bat plane slowly and followed them toward the east. The other bat planes should be out by now. Yes, there was one. He could see it in the moonlight a half mile off.

Presently, a flare burst above it. Two Spads darted down, straight for the eyes of the brute. Vickers rattled. Down, down, streaked Nippy and Bull with deadly aim.

Even before that bat plane wavered, G-8 made out the third one a mile or so behind. The flare brought it out plainly in a hazy blue-moon sky.

THE BAT STAFFEL

The Spads zoomed as the bat plane started falling. Down, down it plunged across the five thousand feet that separated it from the earth, and the people of it that this same bat had cursed the night before.

The last bat plane seemed to sense the danger. It turned lumberingly back for the cave. But two flares burst out. Nippy and Bull pounced upon that last monster like sparrows on a night hawk.

They wheeled and roared in from the front. Vickers rattled their hatred. The flares showed the tracer ribbons slashing into both the eye cockpits of the monster.

The great plane wheeled on one jointed wing. It hung there in the weirdly lighted sky for what seemed like a long time; then it plunged for the earth, turning round and round with sickening leisure.

G-8 glanced at his wrist watch. A thrill shot up his spine. It was after two o'clock in the morning. Most of those hundred thousand German soldiers would be in the tunnel by now, at the north end.

The Spads roared close to him again. Looking for their orders. Again the motors were cut. Bull glided by first. G-8 stood up in his cockpit and shouted.

"Going back with this thing. Going inside and turn on the gas. Be ready for me when I come out."

Bull flew on out of hearing. Nippy came sailing by. G-8 repeated the order. Both looked puzzled, and nodded unwillingly. G-8 grinned as he waved.

He turned the giant plane back toward the spot, fifteen miles away, from which it had come. It wasn't likely that the Boches had seen the activity from there.

He tried to remember every detail of what *Kapitan* Muzzen had told him of the landing device. His two Mercedes motors on full blast, he flew past the front of the mountain once. This should be the correct signal. If he was wrong—But he wasn't!

The great doors opened. On the moonlight he saw the steel arm swing out. The cable dropped. Now for the landing. The interior of the cave was totally dark.

He brought the bat plane down to a fair landing. As it rolled across the rocky floor of the plateau, he felt a jerk. That would be the hook catching. It should be, at least.

It seemed to be. The plane stopped with a jolt and suddenly G-8 felt himself being snapped into the air. The ship tipped, so that his safety belt partly held him in the seat. There was the grinding of machinery. The wings had folded against the thick body.

SUDDENLY, AFTER a grating sound, lights flashed on. Men were standing far below. G-8 was back among the enemy— and by his own free will. His work wasn't finished.

Climbing out of his cockpit, he glanced about quickly. Through his goggles he sighted the switch that he had seen pulled when the Bat machine had carried him out—a prisoner—an hour before. That switch would open the doors, then.

He spotted the German *offizier* in command of the opening and closing. He rushed down the ladder and saluted.

"There has been a little trouble, *Excellenz*," he said. "The other

THE BAT STAFFEL

bats will want to come in quickly. It would be well to open the doors at once and turn out the lights."

The *offizier* hesitated for an instant, stared at G-8 who still wore his helmet and goggles—then nodded.

"*Danke!*" He spun round and shouted orders.

The lights went out. Once more the great door opened.

G-8 leaped for the tanks of gas. Taking a deep breath, he spun the valve of the closest one. A hissing sound told him that the gas was pouring out. He shot his hand to the next valve.

But someone was shooting now. Someone bellowed an order to shut the doors—To switch on the light.

"That is not the pilot of the bat machine," another voice bellowed.

G-8 held his breath. Gas was all about him. One after another, he opened the valves and let them hiss their poison throughout the cave.

He held one hand over his nose and mouth now while he worked on. He was dying for a breath of fresh air.

Bam! The lights flashed on. G-8 turned two more valves wide open, let them hiss. Shouts came from everywhere. Then out of the bedlam, someone yelled.

"*Gott im Himmel!* The gas!"

Lugers flashed!

G-8 ducked double and raced for the open door. Germans were running for it behind him. He reached the switch. Three slugs, hurriedly aimed, crashed past him and were buried in the wall.

A German, unarmed, leaped upon G-8. They rolled together. The Boche was a big, heavy fellow.

G-8 slid out from under him, got an arm lock and rolled him groaning. Then he leaped again for that door switch. Gas was filling the space now. G-8's lungs were bursting, but he didn't dare breathe.

The slab door was closing rapidly. From outside came the drone of two Spads. Germans leaped for G-8 and fell back. Others whom the gas had not reached came on.

G-8 felt dizzy. He reeled as a Luger slug plucked at his arm. He reeled and fell.

CHAPTER 20
HELL HOLE

G-8 WAS not dizzy from taking gas into his lungs. He knew the penalty for that act. But to go through hectic action for nearly two full minutes without allowing himself to take a breath was nearly as bad.

As he fell, a gust of air crossed the narrowing crack of the closing door and blew over him. He chanced a half breath. Guessed right.

He was on his feet again, but unsteadily. He lurched through the ten-foot space that was left for passage. Germans tried to follow. Struggled to keep going, to fight the gas of their own making until they could get past that door and out into fresh air.

But they had done their work well. The gas was deadly to

THE BAT STAFFEL

the highest degree. German soldiers and men slumped to the floor as G-8 staggered through the space, reached the outside.

Clack! The great slab of stone snapped into place once more. The trap was sprung, at least on the one end.

Outside, G-8 stumbled and fell flat on the rocky plateau. His lungs were bursting for air. His breath came in great gasps. Things were blurred about him. He heard the Spads roar down as from a great distance.

He heard their roar die to an idling sound. They would be coming down to land now. Landing for him.

Panting, he staggered to his feet. Bull was coming in first to land. Nippy was close behind. Their wheels touched and rolled. The two Spads stopped within a hundred feet of where G-8 stood, unsteadily grinning at the pilots as they leaped from their cockpits.

"You're hurt," Bull exclaimed. "Look! Your arm's all blood."

G-8 glanced at his bloody sleeve. He moved his arm as proof. Pulled up his sleeve and glanced at the wound. Took a deep breath to satisfy his lung's craving for more air.

"Just a Luger slug," he said. "It'll be all right until we get the rest of our job finished."

Nippy and Bull stared at him.

"Rest of the job?"

"Yes," G-8 nodded. "I turned on as many tanks of gas as I could back there. Their ventilators are right above those tanks. It'll blow that deadly gas right through the tunnel. There's a hundred thousand Germans coming in at the other end. They must be already in at the north end of the tunnel. Word may be telephoned by some of those poor devils before they die that the gas is coming. We'll have to fly up there and stop them."

G-8 was walking toward Nippy's Spad 13.

"Still lucky?" he grinned.

Nippy nodded.

"Is for me so far. Taxi, mister?"

"Yes," said G-8, "but you can fly her this time. I want to lie out here on the side porch and get more air. Phew!"

Hissos roared. The Spads raced across the rocky paving and took the air. As they rose, the closed door of stone gave mute evidence of the deadly effect of the gas within the cave of the bats.

A FEW minutes later they dropped through the moonlit slash of canyon wall and landed. A light appeared at the door of the cabin. Battle, with a flashlight in his hand and his body partially covered with an old-fashioned night shirt, stood blinking at them sleepily.

In his other hand he held one of the oxygen masks. He raised it to his face and called in a husky, guarded voice.

"I say, sir, is it time to put this blasted thing on, sir? Are the bats coming, sir?"

G-8 slipped from the lower wing of Nippy's Spad and laughed.

"I don't think you'll have to wear that thing from now on, Battle," he told him. "The bats are about finished."

"Finished, sir?" he gasped. "If I may say so, sir, that's good news, sir, what?"

"Right, Battle," G-8 shot back. "But it isn't time to celebrate yet. Get your feet in some slippers and help us load our three crates with bombs."

"Bombs, sir?" Battle exploded as he came out with his carpet slippers on. "But I thought you said the bats wouldn't bother you any more and now you're going bombing them, eh?"

"No, Battle, not the bats," G-8 laughed. "We're going to bomb a hole in the ground."

"A hole in the ground," Battle exclaimed. "But I say."

"Better not," G-8 cut in. "We haven't got time to listen right now. Let's get these bombs in the racks and the tanks filled."

All four men hurriedly prepared for the raid. Bull groaned as he carried an armful of bombs beside G-8.

"Don't like this sort of stuff," he ventured. "Like slaughter. Blowing up the end of a tunnel so a hundred thousand poor devils can't get out."

"Right," G-8 admitted. "But it's war. We've got to stop them or they'll kill every man, woman and child in France and more. They're desperate now. They think it's a swell joke. This gas death."

He glanced up at the slit of dark gray above the canyon floor.

"It won't be any cinch though," he added. "It'll be daylight, or nearly so by the time we strike the north entrance of the tunnel."

The three Hissos warmed. Three pilots inspected their craft by flashlight. Guns blasted. G-8 first, then Bull and, last, Nippy thundered out of the canyon bottom and climbed through the top. The moon had gone down. A dull, gray mist enveloped them—or so the darkness seemed in that moment before light.

As G-8 banked and swung north he let out the aerial wire from the bottom of his Spad. His fingers began tapping the key at the side of his cockpit. Steadily he ticked out the message in code and repeated it as he led his Battle Aces northward.

> Move all available squadrons to Belfort and hold ready with warmed engines. Have troops and tanks ready to move from Mulhouse. Bat menace over. Going now to cork up Tunnel with plenty of Germans. Will leave way clear.
> G-8.

He reeled in his aerial once more.

The gray in the east was growing lighter as a warning of the coming day. G-8 surveyed the ground below from an altitude of three thousand feet. He could make out landmarks in the dim light. He spotted the island where he had entered the lateral tunnel; they droned over it a few minutes later. Turned to Freiburg.

Below, thick woods looked soft. Breaks in the trees here and there showed places where fresh earth had been dumped in great heaps. There, within a radius of a thousand feet, the exact entrance to the tunnel must be. He couldn't make it out. Perhaps when the day broke more clearly.

He circled again. Climbed. Came up suddenly at a shadow passing close to his wing. Nippy had pulled his Spad ahead out of formation and was waving wildly.

G-8's attention for the moment had been on the tree tops far below. And so he hadn't noticed a group of black specks coming out of the west.

THE BAT STAFFEL

From an upside down position, G-8 saw two Fokkers clinging to his tail.

His teeth clenched for an instant. His work was practically finished, yet so far from being done! They must make their victory complete. The *Herr Doktor* Krueger, devil of all clever devils, had the secret of the gas. Knew how to make more. Would not hesitate to do so if he could continue to have the permission of those in high command.

So this must be a total routing of the German forces in this sector. The slaughter must be terrible to make the High Command realize that the Bat gas must not be used. Make them see that it could be turned against them as well as to their advantage.

FRANTICALLY, G-8 searched the tree tops for the exact opening of the tunnel. He must find it and bomb it shut before those Boche planes reached them. Must be—yes, there were. Nine in that flight. They were Fokkers, coming like vengeful eagles.

G-8 continued to search the tree tops. Wherever the tunnel mouth was, it was cleverly camouflaged with trees. The Fokkers were screaming nearer. He heard their warning bursts as they pressed nine triggers and eighteen Spandau guns stuttered and raved.

G-8 shot his fist up instantly. No time to dodge now. They'd have to fight it out. No cinch, fighting nine Fokkers with three Spads. Spads that were weighed down with a full load of bombs.

G-8 flipped the tail of his Spad, banked and hurled straight for the snarling Boches. Guns belched. Vickers spat to warm. Nippy and Bull were even with him, flying with Hissos screaming in a wild lunge.

THE BAT STAFFEL

Each Spad pilot crouched behind his guns and stared across his sights. Teeth were clenched. Hold until you either crash or they give way. That was G-8's determination. The Fokkers would have to crash them or swerve. He guessed they would swerve.

Nearer and nearer. It seemed that those planes racing head on had no space, no time to turn from their course before they tangled in death.

Several German guns spoke. G-8 grinned. That was a good sign. A sign that the pilots were nervous. That they wouldn't hold to the last split second.

The first one to turn was the leader of the Fokker flight. The instant he did so, G-8 pressed his triggers. Other Fokkers plunged. Some zoomed.

The lead Fokker swerved again—downward this time. The pilot had tipped forward in his bucket seat, with a bullet in his head from the guns of G-8. As he spun, another diving Fokker locked wings with it.

Down, down they plunged together. Down for the wood below.

Nippy sent a Fokker down. Bull missed and turned to get his man on a second burst. Two Fokkers jumped his tail. It was slow maneuvering those Spads with their loads of bombs.

G-8 kicked and jerked the stick. His Spad whirled and zoomed up sluggishly as Bull tried to roll out of his trouble. But his ship was too heavily loaded. The Fokkers caught him in their cross-fire. Yellow tracers muddied the clear morning sky and slashed through his tail group. They crept up on the cockpit where Bull fought to pull out.

G-8 glared across his sights. Pressed the trigger button. His Vickers chattered and sent their white tracer ribbons fluffing into the cockpit of one Fokker.

He kicked the nose toward the other. He was literally hanging on his prop. Funny how these fully-loaded Spads changed so completely with more weight put upon them.

The movement of the rudder was sluggish. The Hisso was grinding with a deep-throated moan. The Fokker pilot who remained on Bull's tail turned a white face toward G-8. He saw his trouble. Kicked over to get out.

But G-8, nose in the air, sticking up in a stall for a last shot at that Fokker pilot, nailed him where he rolled.

Down, down tore the Fokker at the end of a long smoke and flame column, twisting as it fell.

G-8 moved the controls. Nothing happened.

Tac-tac-tac!

From beneath, Spandau guns rattled up at him. For once in his life his eagerness for a kill had placed him in a dead spot. He hadn't, for the moment, counted on the overloading of his Spad. He would have been all right except for that load of bombs. Couldn't drop them now. Not until be found the opening of the tunnel—if that time ever came.

Yellow tracers slashed through the covering of his stalled Spad. German steel drummed. Controls flapped. He seemed helpless.

THE BAT STAFFEL

CHAPTER 21
VENGEANCE SKY GUNS

IN DESPERATION, G-8 whirled and stared behind him. Three Fokkers were snarling, up on his tail. Three Fokkers with flame-penciled guns and yellow tracers flicked from their muzzles.

Drummmm! Holes appeared in the right wing. Stitched along toward the cockpit.

G-8 shot his stick ahead and kicked the rudder to the left. His heavily loaded Spad began to fall on that side. The Fokkers streaked after him.

Then, combined with that rattle of Spandau guns, he heard the chatter of Vickers behind. His Spad was falling. The Hisso had ceased to groan; it was running wild. But the three Fokkers were fighting desperately to get in that fatal shot.

Tac-tac-tac! G-8 yanked his stick cautiously this time. From an upside down position he saw two of the Fokkers still clinging to his tail. They had followed him over easily. Nippy and Bull were both roaring after them. The third Fokker was going down, nose first.

Bull's gun sent another one down. G-8 kicked out in a roll and slammed down on the third. He glared across his sights, pressed his trigger button and sent death and destruction slashing into that Fokker cockpit.

His Spad bucked and leaped about in the air. Archie had gone crazy down there among the trees. Yellow bursts appeared everywhere. A hail of flying steel slashed the air, made it whine with speed.

The air seemed suddenly clear of Fokkers. Those that remained able to fly had taken to retreat. They were roaring back toward the west.

G-8 glanced down, flying constantly his zigzag course. His eyes nearly popped out of his head. Bull and Nippy came in close. G-8 was pointing down. They nodded. Archie was making their planes dance about like three phantom dolls on a string.

Below, flames licked upward from a burning wreck. And about the flames, men ran. Men trying to get into the flames and through them, it seemed. No, they were trying to put out the flames.

Instantly, G-8 saw the reason. Beside that flaming wreckage he could make out a great hole in the ground. The plane in crashing had torn several trees down with it, leaving an opening that he could now see through.

The north end of the tunnel. Bull and Nippy nodded.

Noses dropped. Hissos whined. And now ground machine guns joined in the bedlam of noise and flying steel.

Spads whirled and came on down. They strung out, one behind the other. G-8 first, Bull next and Nippy last.

Down, down in a twisted course. Hissos screamed with their driving speed. Vickers guns rattled back at the ground crews as they blasted up.

Then over the spot where the planes burned and the trees were torn away, showing the mouth of the north end of the

THE BAT STAFFEL

tunnel. Down low over the trees they romped, where machine guns and archie could not see to take aim.

G-8 flashed his hand down in a signal to drop the bombs. He roared over the place. His hand reached for the bomb toggles and he pulled twice in rapid succession as he stared over the side to gauge his aim at the low altitude.

Blam! Blam!

He whirled in his seat, saw Bull thundering down behind him. More explosions from Bull's bombs. Then Nippy came slashing in from the side, in a steep roaring bank like a snapping terrier, and dropped bombs.

G-8 WAS already hurling back over the spot. He looked down. A few men were running; others were lying dead about the spot that had been the opening to the tunnel.

Two, three Germans were dragging themselves out of a small hole that was left. G-8 pointed. The cork must be inserted all of the way. The cave-in must be complete.

Again he pulled on his toggle lever. But this time he pulled only once. Something, perhaps a subconscious plan stopped him. He had six bombs all together. Had had when he had started. Now he had three left.

He whirled in his seat as he saw his bomb miss the opening that was left by a few feet. He pointed it out as Bull roared down. Saw Bull nod.

Blam! The ground heaved and spouted skyward. And almost at the same instant Nippy's Spad 13 screamed down and let go with his load.

G-8 was back over the place again. He nodded. Waved his

G-8 AND HIS BATTLE ACES

hand to signal for the finish. Like the three bongs of a small town fire bell telling that the fire was over.

And as he waved and saw them get the idea, he saw Nippy pointing into the west. G-8 whirled and stared. The sky seemed black with planes. Enemy planes they must be. They were coming out of the heart of Germany.

For only an instant, G-8 paused in his decision. Victory must be decisive or it was no victory to G-8. At the same instant he saw far to the west, straight in the path of the coming jagdstaffels of enemy planes the proud tower of Freiburg castle. The castle where the fiend, *Herr Doktor* Krueger had been. Where he would be, beyond doubt. And seeing the castle he thought of the three bombs he had saved—for that express purpose.

He spun in his seat and glanced at Bull and Nippy. They thundered on either side of him. Seemed anxious and eager to take on the fight. G-8 waved nonchalantly back and grinned. He let the aerial spin out below his Spad once more. Began ticking another code message on the key beside him.

TUNNEL CORKED. COME RUNNING TO HOLD THE POSITIONS WE ARE MAKING POSSIBLE. TANKS. BOMBERS. PURSUITS. INFANTRY. ARTILLERY.

G-8

Over and over again he repeated that message until the triple flight of Fokkers were almost upon them.

He reeled in his cable aerial and pressed his triggers calmly to warm his guns once more. His eyes took in everything. He'd

THE BAT STAFFEL

have to pass through that mass of Fokkers, through or around them to come over Freiburg Castle to bomb it. Three bombs should be enough and plenty to blast the castle and kill the little devil *doktor*. And three bombs were still just enough to make his Spad difficult to handle in a tight dogfight.

His decision was quick. The Fokkers were still out of range. The rattle of warning Spandau guns, many guns, came to him, Nippy and Bull answered with their flame-tipped Vickers.

G-8 whirled in his seat and pointed Nippy and Bull to hold the same level as he stuck his own nose upward and began to climb.

The Fokkers, whirling at them at four miles a minute and more, seemed to hesitate when G-8 leaped his Spad in the air and shot upward.

Five of the Fokkers, a whole flight, detached from the rest and snarled up at G-8 and his Spad. Higher and higher he climbed. The trick must be perfect.

They were almost within range now. G-8 nipped the controls.

Tac-tac-tac! Spandaus rattled from below as Fokkers hung on their props and fired at him. That was part of it. Now for the trick that would tell—

Down went the nose of the Spad. It began to plunge and then to spin dizzily. Around and around and around. And ahead of G-8, Freiburg Castle spun.

His left wing nearly nicked a Fokker tail as he tore down. He didn't have to turn and look up to see that all the Fokkers, taken by surprise, were above him now. He also knew without twisting his neck that they had seen his purpose, were all coming down at him.

Down, down with full gun. He yanked out of his spin to get more speed. There would be more danger that way, but—

Fokkers with their longer dive had more speed and gained. Spandaus guns rattled and behind, Nippy and Bull lunged down in their Spads with flaming Vickers.

A race with death. Fokkers stopping a Spad. Two Spads trying to stop nearly ten times as many Fokkers.

A boom told of a bursted gas tank. G-8 spun and stared. A Fokker was flaming down in the mass.

He jerked out of his dive just as Freiburg Castle tower stormed up at him. Barely in time too. Mercedes whined and groaned.

G-8 had his hand on the bomb toggle lever. He pulled once. Must make sure of his shots.

Blam! The tower went up in a spray of rocks and dust. Instantly he pulled around and roared back.

Yellow tracers slashed through his right wing. Drummed on his turtle back covering. His instrument board vanished and hot oil blinded him for the moment.

SOMEHOW HE managed to make that turn and come back. This time he could take no more chances. Oil line gone. Motor would be done before long.

He pulled twice in rapid succession on the bomb lever.

Blam! Blam!

The main part of the ancient Freiburg Castle erupted into the air and fell with a roar that G-8 could hear even above the thunder of his Hisso.

THE BAT STAFFEL

Fokkers all about him. He had taken a desperate chance and won—for the moment.

But the winning seemed about to turn into losing of his own life the next instant. Yellow tracers fluffed about him in a sulphurous haze. The Hisso that had been screaming a split second before, stopped with a grunt and died.

A Fokker stormed down past G-8 and its pilot pointed toward the field which G-8 had used after his escape from the castle.

Nothing else to do. A warning burst of Spandau slugs slashed through his left wing. His ship covering was riddled with bullets. Astonishing how it held together at all.

G-8 waved his understanding to the German pilot and smiled. So this was the end.

Behind he heard the rattle of Spandau guns and Vickers. He turned in his cockpit. Wanted to shout, to cheer Nippy and Bull as they slashed about at other Fokkers.

One, two, three Fokkers curled up and sizzled earthward while G-8 glided to land. Another Fokker tore down out of control. Nippy and Bull were fighting now like wild men. Their guns scarcely ceased to fire at all. They must be white-hot. Any instant they would jam from overheating. Still another and then another Fokker stormed down, the two crashing in the air as they tangled to get out of the way of the two demons in Spads 13 and 7.

The wheels of G-8's Spad touched ground and rolled. Funny to end life at the same place where the episode of the bats had

G-8 AND HIS BATTLE ACES

started. But at any rate he wouldn't be shot before that castle wall. That wall wasn't there now.

He leaped from the cockpit as Germans came running across the field. He ducked under the Hisso for protection and let go with his Luger. Fokkers from above saw what went on and tried to stab him in his hiding place. Spandau slugs clanked and pinged and ricocheted from the Hisso. One grazed his ear. He ducked.

Nippy was desperately trying to slam about and get in for a landing, An entirely hopeless affair. Once he cut his gun and glided down straight, Fokker's would be upon his tail, crucifying him to his cockpit.

G-8 gasped. He shouted a warning Nippy couldn't hear.

He stopped short, clutched the bottom of the Hisso cowling and watched for an instant. Nippy was coming in to land. There were still almost two complete flights of Fokkers in the air swarming like bees. But Nippy was coming just the same. Coming to land. To save G-8, a pal of short duration—but a pal.

And while he glided down, Bull seemed to have gone crazy. G-8 blasted at a German who sneaked through the grass toward him and stared up again open mouthed. It was hard to believe that any plane could go through the maneuvers that Bull was forcing his Spad number 7 to do.

But it was futile. Three Fokkers broke away, got out of range of Bull's guns while the remaining Fokkers kept him very busy indeed, and slammed down on Nippy's tail.

G-8 ducked from his cover. Pointed. Shouted. Nippy turned.

THE BAT STAFFEL

Instantly, he saw his danger. His Hisso blasted and he looked to one side and prepared to take the air again.

All that in a split second. His opening the gun. His staring into the south. His eyes popping and his pointing.

G-8 whirled. His eyes too popped. They must have been ready. Got his message. The sky was almost black with squadron after squadron of Allied planes. Nieuports, S. E.s, Bristols, D. H.s, Spads, Camels.

He heard Nippy's engine die again. Heard him landing. Somehow the gun fire from above had ceased abruptly. G-8 turned. The remaining Fokkers were in plenty hurry for retreat.

Nippy's Spad 13 was rolling past. G-8 leaped from his crippled Spad and flattened on the lower right wing. Spad 13 whirled, taxied hurriedly to the end of the field and roared into the wind.

CHAPTER 22
VICTORY WINGS

AS THEY thundered into the air G-8, from his position on the wing with the wind ripping at his clothing, pointed toward the great squadrons of Allied planes that were roaring into Germany above them.

There were heavy bombers far to the southwest. And below them the earth heaved as their bombs wrecked the ground.

"They'll hold plenty now," G-8 shouted to Nippy over the cowling. "Heinie had every available man in this sector in the tunnel. Look—"

He pointed on beyond the eastern lines now where the line came down near Switzerland in the mountains. He turned to Bull flying tip to tip with Nippy's Spad, and Bull grinned and nodded that he saw too.

Row upon row of great tanks moved like mechanical ants far below, south of that line that the big bombers had just blasted.

Pursuits were picking off every German they could see behind the lines. Yank pursuits and French on that end.

G-8 watched with a satisfied smile frozen on his face. Then they were banking into the slit of a canyon.

G-8 dropped from the wing when they landed. Bull's Spad number 7 rolled to a stop beside them. G-8 stretched and stifled a yawn.

A voice came from the door of the cabin. A matter of fact voice.

"If I may say so, sir, your breakfast is getting cold, sir."

Battle was walking toward them from the cabin. He surveyed the bullet-riddled Spads, and looked a bit puzzled at his master.

"And if I might add, sir, this hardly looks like the beginning of a vacation in the mountains you mentioned back at Le Bourget."

G-8 laughed.

"That vacation is starting about now for a while. And we'll begin by eating that breakfast you mentioned, Battle. Let's go, men."

All three were hungry. They talked of the fight here and there between mouths full of ham and eggs. Then chairs were pushed back and cigarettes were lighted.

G-8 grew serious for the moment.

"Perhaps you men have been wondering what this is all about, this hook-up between you and me?" he said.

Nippy nodded.

"Couldn't help wondering just where we went from here," he confessed.

"I suppose," Bull suggested fearfully, "now that the job is finished we'll be shot back to our outfits. That would seem pretty tame after what we've just been through."

G-8 smiled.

"Sort of like the vacation Battle's been talking about, eh?" he said. "Well that was the original idea I guess, but I think I'll have it changed. The big chief himself has made me a special agent of the Secret Service. I picked you to help with this job. It's been swell being together. I can see no reason why we shouldn't make this a regular outfit The three of us and Battle. We'll likely have a lot of fun and—" he added with a grin: "we might help the good old U.S.A. win the war, just as a side line. My headquarters are in the end hangar at Le Bourget Field. We'll have the place enlarged to accommodate everybody. Take the whole hangar if necessary. How's that strike you?"

"Swell," chirped Nippy.

Bull seemed to be having more difficulty in expressing his deep feeling. His eyes were misty. As usual, the big, two fisted brutish looking one had the softest, most sentimental heart of the three.

"Ok-ay," he choked.

Nippy winked at G-8.

"Bull gets feathers in his eyes easy," he grinned. "From being chicken-hearted."

Bull growled and lunged for his little pal. But Nippy ducked and came around to G-8's side of the table.

FROM HIS pocket G-8 had taken a well-worn note book. He ran through the pages, found the next blank one and began to write.

Nippy looked over his shoulder and asked:

"What's that, your home work? Thought you said this was recess."

The master spy laughed.

"Not quite," he said. "It's my diary. I keep a diary of everything that happens. War diary. Thought some of the gang back home might get a kick out of it after this fuss is over. Then, too, there's a lot of things I don't want to forget."

"That's a swell idea," Bull agreed a bit snuffily. "Maybe I'll keep a diary too from now on."

From the safe distance behind the table. Nippy grinned and emitted a well-ripened razzberry in sound effect.

"You?" he cracked. "You wouldn't have anything to put in it even if you could write, you, big ox."

G-8 laughed again. Then he grew serious and his pencil poised over the blank page.

"I wish," he mused, "I could write down that *Herr Doktor* Krueger was turned to dust by his own gas but I suppose instead

THE BAT STAFFEL

I'll have to put down the thing that is more likely. That he was killed when I bombed his headquarters, Freiburg castle."

Nippy laughed.

"You must think he's crazy if you figure he'd take a chance of getting trapped in that tunnel," he said.

"I do," G-8 answered. "I think most great geniuses like Krueger are crazy along some lines. If you could have seen that bird as I saw him you'd think he was pretty crazy."

"Begging your pardon, sir," Battle interrupted, "do you mean to suggest, sir, that a clever chap like *Doktor* Krueger could be a bit daft as we say, sir."

"Right," laughed G-8. "Call it daft or crazy or nuts or bats. It all means sick in the bean. Rattly rafters. Loose upstairs."

Battle blinked.

"Rafters? Upstairs, sir? Bats, sir? Haw-haw-haw."

His face lighted with the slow dawning of an idea.

"I—I believe I get it, sir. Bats. Haw-haw. In the belfry, sir. A joke. Very good, show. You've been joking about the bats all of the time, sir, and I just saw the funny side of it, sir. Imagine, sir?"

"I can't," groaned G-8.

POPULAR PUBLICATIONS
HERO PULPS

LOOK FOR MORE SOON!

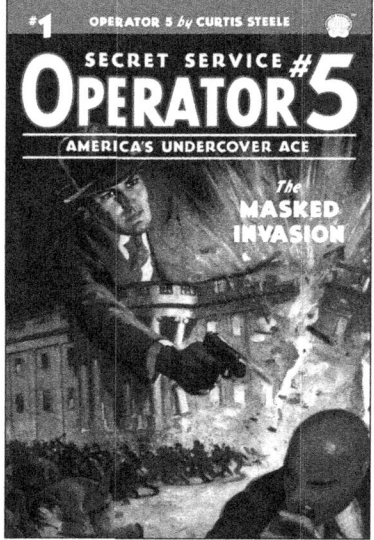

Printed in Great Britain
by Amazon